foreword by
crystal lacey winslow

Lipstick
diaries

a provocative
look into the
female
perspective

edited by
anthony whyte
Author of GHETTO GIRLS SERIES

AUGUSTUS
PUBLISHING

WHERE
**HIP HOP
LITERATURE**
BEGINS...

AUGUSTUS
PUBLISHING

Copyright 2007 Augustus Publishing
ISBN: 0975945394

Edited by Anthony Whyte
Design/Photogaphy: Jason Claiborne

First printing Augustus Publishing paperback May 2007

AugustusPublishing.com
info@augustuspublishng.com

foreword

Talk about a new phenomenon that's taking over our streets, infesting our ghettos and seeping into the minds of our people. I'm not talking about any drug or disease. I'm talking about a new epidemic that's breeding writers. A whole new crop of authors have emerged and are flourishing into major book chains, sitting proudly atop the shelves along with New York Times bestsellers.

Street literature is an outlet of expression for African-American authors. It characterizes to some degree who we are as a race and chronicles our struggles in today's society by incorporating relatable dilemmas and situations. It hits home to most street-lit readers because the storylines are organic and there's an authenticity in the plots. You'll find backdrops of our culture and heritage wedged in the lines of most novels with an underlining message or moral. This new genre, street literature, symbolizes growth and change. It not only strikes a cord with those who have experienced similar situations but it also enlightens those who have not.

I came into the publishing arena as an author who self-published my first novel, *Life, Love & Loneliness*, which originally started out as a poem. I took the title and developed the storyline using my freestyle writing technique. In 2002, *Life, Love & Loneliness* was released and went on to hit the Essence bestseller's list. I've since evolved into a small, boutique publishing company that released the #1 Essence bestseller: *Wifey* and the acclaimed follow up *Still Wifey* amongst other titles.

Many people read my stories and ask if there's any truth to the storylines or characters. I always say no. The truth is, I live vicariously through my characters and each character is a reflection of who I am, where I've traveled, and who I've encountered. There is a certain synergism between myself and my characters that I can't deny. Does that mean that I've torn a page from my life and wrote about it? Absolutely not! All it means is that there's a connection which allows me to write cinematically.

Change and growth are so important. We achieve this by allowing new, fresh voices in the door. I feel that it's my duty to kick open the doors for writers to come behind me and make their own accolades in this business. I put on my baseball cap and tightened up my laces a few years ago in a quest to pave the way for other authors to bum rush the doors. By no means am I saying that I'm a martyr or a pioneer. I am an enthusiastic catalyst for newer voices.

There's been chatter since 2003 that Hip Hop fiction is a fad; that it's not going to last. Naysayers have gone so far as to compare it to black exploitation films in the 1970's. These innuendos are the common thread that's placing doubt, fear and insecurities in most authors thought process. I've observed that this generation of writers is often afraid to let others in because they don't want anyone else to share the glory. Their insecurities overshadow their judgment. My belief is that you'll always get what your hands call for. There is enough room in the publishing arena for everyone. If you are truly talented; you'll sustain. So shake the tree and the weak branches will fall.

The Lipstick Diaries is composed by an eclectic group of authors. Some stories have poignant, heartfelt storylines while others are raw and gritty. Either way, it's an adventurous read. And you won't know unless you give it a chance. I'm asking that you trust me and be prepared to stimulate your mind while reading through each story laced with sex, controversy and scandal. And who better to tell the tales?

Did I mention *The Lipstick Diaries* is authored by a strong all women ensemble? Enough said…

setting sun
Justice Mejia

Come,

Meet with me

At the place they call warm

Plush, soft, and strong

Show me how

You differ; vices, virtues

likes and dislikes

Guide my time, your past

Meet me at happiness

Support, comfort and all

Meet me at changes

Growth and despair

Drench me in laughter

Experience and travel

Gallivant with me

In sand, water and moon

Come -

Meet with me

At success, expansion

Birth and family

Meet me at Love.

"Do you love me enough to move to Boston?" he asked.

My eyes widened, the pen dropped from my fingers and I closed the book of poetry. We loved each other but I didn't think someone actually wanted me for me. The trepidation was overwhelming.

"Can I have a little time to think it over?" I asked struggling with my thoughts.

My heart pounded loudly. I really wanted to say yes. The past had taught me that anything life changing was worth some thinking. I sipped cranberry with vodka and nestled my trembling body in the warmth of his multi-colored velvet blanket. Sebastian was painting a picture on a white canvas. I was eager to see the outcome of the fiery, red paint he was using but after couple sips, I fell fast asleep.

The following morning I awoke and could hear him humming in the shower. I was still in the throes of stretching and yawning when I glanced up at it. The canvas was complete. I stared speculating what it was.

I moved in for a closer look. Shapes appeared like the leaves of a jungle tree, forming three-dimensionally the longer I stared. I admired, then stepped back and noticed the painting seemed even redder. It's like the setting sun, I thought.

Sebastian finished his shower. He joined me, hugged and kissed me softly.

"Good morning, my love, did you sleep well?" he asked.

"Yes," I replied blushing and turning my focus on him.

"It's for you," he smiled and drew me closer. "You've always wanted me to paint something for you. I watched you sleep and that's my inspiration. You're beautiful, the sunset of my life that's captured in painting," he said pointing to the canvas. Rapture rushed me when I saw his gallant smile.

"Thank you baby," I replied staring in his eyes. The proposal for Boston reappeared and I turned away.

I walked to the bathroom thinking how I'd met Sebastian. We were criminal justice majors and shared the same uncertainty about what we really wanted to do. I was leaning towards becoming a lawyer but changed my mind. I wanted to keep all options opened.

Two years after we met, Sebastian was offered an incredible opportunity with a law firm in Boston. It was our senior year and they wanted him to start after graduation. Our relationship was nothing short of spectacular. Romantic and caring, me and my six-foot-one, black hair, light-complexion, Puerto Rican man were wrapped in deep conversations running all day long.

I wasn't one who trusted easily especially the men I dated. Sebastian changed that for me. We had many nights staying up talking about our past. My stories seemed to be littered with the fear of getting hurt. Sebastian helped me realize that getting hurt was par for the course.

"The easiest people to hurt are the ones we love," he said. His strong hands cupped my face. "If you let me into your heart, into your world, sweetheart, I'll protect it forever." Sebastian promised, his eyes probing mine. The passionate kiss that followed was the confirmation; he really cared.

It was a new day and my mind started to wander in class. Professor Smith's lectures were never easy. He spoke in a monotone voice and seemed unaffected that most of his students were doing other work in his class. I started to think of Sebastian and his offer to leave New York.

I enjoyed this city with its vibrant heart. Often I'd find myself in smoke drenched bars, quenching my thirst for nightlife. The beat was loud enough to drill life into you as well as out. Even the bartenders were entertaining while mixing new drinks. It was a show all to its own. Anywhere, at any point one could find a hundred people engaged in different conversations.

My thoughts were adrift when Professor Smith loudly cleared his throat. I realized class was over when my mind washed ashore from an infectious fantasy. Packing my books I left the classroom.

"Hey Justice…" I heard as I walked through the hall.

I turned and saw Elizabeth, who for the last three years

had been a dear, best friend. She was short with strawberry blonde hair and fair complexion, from a small town in Ohio. Elizabeth was naïve and kept me by her side so she wouldn't be swallowed by the big city. She often studied with Sebastian and me. Her parents were well-off and this afforded her the luxury of staying at our college dorm, right in the heart of NY. Her apartment had an amazing view of Central Park.

We were labeled the three musketeers and did everything together. Elizabeth didn't have a boyfriend. Sebastian and I tried not to make her feel like a third wheel.

"I'm starving, do you want to go to our spot and get a bite?" She asked.

I had time before my next class so a bite to eat sounded great. John's deli, our spot where we spent a lot of time, was just up the block. Elizabeth got a pepperoni slice and I got a sausage slice with extra cheese. Midway through our pizza, Sebastian slid next to me. He kissed me and waved at Elizabeth. She blushed. I blamed her fair complexion and the steam from her pizza. She always asked for her slice to be extra hot. Sebastian started with his usual stories. I listened because he had a great sense of humor. He found a way to make any bad day better.

Later on that night we were all at Elizabeth's dorm. I was

so taken by the view of the park. I think I visited her often not just to study but because the view was enticing. My best poems were composed from the inspiration of the view.

"Are you hungry?" Sebastian asked.

I shook my head. Elizabeth and Sebastian were big eaters. They both needed a few hours in the gym. Instead, they ordered Chinese food and were eating while I started on a brief that needed to be fifty pages long. It was due tomorrow which meant it was going to be a long night. Elizabeth put on a cute playboy sleepwear. I thought it a little too short but I didn't say anything. Sebastian changed into his boxers and T-shirt. I changed into my usual gray sweats.

We were close and talked about everything. We had a lot of the same classes together, but Elizabeth and Sebastian had classes that I didn't. Sebastian helped Elizabeth with her papers. At times I assisted them.

When Elizabeth fell asleep, Sebastian caressed my shoulders and neck. I loved the touch of his strong hands. He kissed me and we got busy with the linguistics of his tongue. I still had about twenty pages left to write.

"Sorry, baby but I really need to finish doing this. Tomorrow after work, pick me up at the store and we'll go to

Brooklyn. I'll make this up to you." I said kissing him softly.

"Okay, good night baby," he said.

He went and slipped into the bed leaving me room when I was ready to join him. Elizabeth slept on a make shift bed on the floor. How lucky I was to have them both? I thought as I stayed up to finish my paper.

My parents raised me to be independent. I was an honor student all of my academic years and got leadership awards from various clubs in high school. Even now while working two jobs to pay for school, I still found time to participate in the student council government and other clubs.

I worked in retail because the hours were flexible and I received great discounts. I worked at nightclubs on weekends. I was dancing before I actually walked. I wouldn't be able to breathe if ever I felt I couldn't dance. My friends came to see me work my thing at Webster Hall, Velvet, Expo and Limelight. I loved the life and the ability to make others smile from watching me dance. I was raised in a strict home and dancing in some of the hottest clubs in NYC was my release.

The heavy schedule of school and work made me exhausted. I eagerly waited to see Sebastian walk in the store. The minutes dragged. I was beaming when Sebastian came in carrying the most beautiful sunflowers. He handed me the bouquet.

"Thank you baby," I said with a smile wider than any seen in toothpaste commercials. "I'll be out in a few minutes, meet me by the employee exit." I quickly signed out and proceeded to be checked by security.

I hugged Sebastian tightly as butterflies fluttered in my stomach. Finally I'd met the right person.

"Are we going straight home, baby?"

The question snapped my drifting thoughts.

"Yes!" I replied.

No papers to write tonight, I couldn't wait to get home and have a quiet evening at home with my boyfriend. When we arrived, I dropped my purse on the table and looked for the vase. Of course there were none in his bachelor pad. I made use of an empty bottle and put my sunflowers in water. Sebastian stood behind me and slowly kissed the back of my neck. He took my hand and extended it outward to the side until our fingertips met.

"I love you. Come with me." He whispered.

I faced him and kissed him. He wanted to say more but I put my index finger across his lips. Our lips stayed locked and

I became lost. There was nothing wrong in the world. We were now intertwined between the sheets. Soon he'd warmed me up from the slight chill of fall in full bloom.

Sebastian slipped inside of me. My fingers clawed the air. I needed to hold on to something. The anger of his deep, pelvic thrusts was unmatched. Spreading my legs wider, I relaxed and gave in to his wrath. Beads of sweat formed between his chest and mine. He sucked my lips, his drink of love intoxicating me. My body collapsed in pleasure and I drifted into sleep.

The next morning, I awoke by his side. Despite the prospect of a long day ahead of me, I snuggled in his arms. Friday, I had classes and the club later in the night. I also needed to come up with a plan for his birthday the following week. I jumped up, got dressed, stuffed a bagel in my mouth and kissed him goodbye. Lucky for him, his first class wasn't until the afternoon. He was on full scholarship and didn't have to work so he could sleep in. Besides time with me, Sebastian spent a lot of his spare time painting and attending various club meetings.

At around noon, I met up with Elizabeth at our spot after breezing through my morning.

"What do you think I should do for Sebastian's birthday? It's next Thursday."

She blotted the grease off her pizza with a napkin then looked up at me with a pensive look.

"I don't know. You know him best." She responded in a tone that sounded like I was bothering her.

"Are you ok Lizzie?" I asked.

"I'm fine!"

It didn't sound like she was but I left it alone. I was almost done with my chicken cutlet sandwich. Elizabeth had already polished off her pizza.

"Studying famous trials and recreating mock juries is such a great learning experience." I said as we rushed off to one of the classes Elizabeth and I shared.

After the class I headed home. I wanted to take a nap before work. I called Sebastian as I usually do. We discussed our day. Our schedules were opposite on Fridays. He always mentioned missing me. I got home, fell in a great nap and dreamt about exactly what I was going to do for Sebastian's birthday.

I awoke at nine pm and had to be at the club by eleven. I jumped in the shower, changed and raced out the door to catch the train. By the time I had arrived, the club was packed as usual. I walked around greeting all the staff and fellow dancers. Working together was so much fun. I was scheduled for three forty-five minute sets and the rest of the time I could party.

I'm not certain if it was the music or the feel of my new fishnets, but something kept the smile on my face. The night was especially vibrant. My first set took place on the main floor. I was dancing on a platform where ropes hung from the ceiling. I twirled the rope a few times, jumped on and rolled with it as it unwound. The red silk bra and short black Lycra shorts I wore not only made me feel sexy, but also outlined my assets.

The night progressed with a few vodka shots during my break. I felt even more energy to dance. I hit the dance floor and battled other dancers. I was on top of my game and in my own world when I was dancing.

Four a.m. came quickly. I clocked out, changed and pulled out some money for a cab. Exhausted, I arrived home at five and immediately fell asleep.

Saturday I awoke to my ringing phone. It was Sebastian asking if he could come over. I told him yes. He could help me run some errands in the neighborhood and I reminded him I was working tonight. In the bathroom, I realized he hadn't called me at five this morning. He always called to check if I got home okay. Sebastian probably was just too tired to wake up and call, I thought brushing it off.

We lived only a few train stops away from each other and Sebastian was ringing the doorbell. I opened the door and he scooped me up, swinging me around while giving me a great hug.

"I missed you last night. How was the club?" he asked.

"Amazing," I replied smiling. "I made great tips last night. Baby, you didn't call when I got off. What were you up to?"

"I was asleep and didn't set my alarm to call you. I'm sorry," he apologized kissing me.

"That's okay. You never failed before. I guess I got used to it."

We spent the day getting my laundry done. We went grocery shopping and I decided to cook for us both before leaving for work. I made his favorite steak with onions and white rice.

Two hours remained after dinner before I had to go. It was plenty of time for twelve-play. I aggressively slid my hands down his leg heading for his manhood.

"Baby, I'm sorry. I'm kinda tired." He said and stopped me.

My jaw dropped opened with surprise. I thought he was addicted to sex. Sebastian wanted me every chance we had but not today. He decided to leave and I got dressed then escaped to my alter ego. The whole incident replayed mentally as I danced.

Sunday, I slept well into the afternoon. Sebastian hadn't called me at five a.m. I called him when I woke up.

"Baby, how are you?" I asked.

"I'm fine sweetie. How was last night?" he replied hurriedly.

"It was alright. I made even more money than Friday night. What did you get into last night?"

I first wanted to hear what he'd say and chose not to mention the call.

"Baby, I was working on a canvas and really got into it. And then I went out with the boys for some drinks, I got back around four am and feel asleep."

That was totally out of his character. No matter what Sebastian would always call or send me a text. He'd tell me every time he was hanging with the fellows. Sebastian suddenly changed and I didn't know why. Our conversation was going no where fast. I changed the subject by informing him that I was staying at Elizabeth's for the night. He told me he had hoped we could talk about Boston.

I still wasn't ready to answer that question. I hung up,

changed and went to Manhattan. It was a beautiful cool afternoon, the leaves had started to fall and I loved the sound it made when it rustled against my shoes. I got to Elizabeth's dorm and smelled spaghetti sauce from the elevator. She had limited cooking skills. Every time she announced she was cooking we knew exactly what we'd be eating; spaghetti with meat sauce. I got to her door right when she was on her way to the restroom. It was down the hall shared by students on the floor.

"Hi sweetie" I said.

She was frightened but quickly gathered herself and reached out to hug me.

"I'll be right back," she said and she raced down the hall.

I walked into her room and changed into my sweats. I kept a pair at her dorm. When Elizabeth returned, we ate in front of the TV. She showed me some new DVD's and wanted me to pick some to watch while she made popcorn. The popcorn was ready by the time I had picked out the ones I wanted to see. We curled up on the bed and it was girl's movie night. It was fun hanging with Elizabeth. Every once in a while I'd glance at the park.

Sebastian called at ten and we chatted. He told me he had

finished a new painting and wanted to show it to me. We talked and he asked to speak to Elizabeth. They chatted for a minute too long and I was exhausted at this point. Elizabeth handed me the cell phone. I wished Sebastian goodnight and went to sleep until I heard the alarm the following morning.

On Mondays I had a heavy class schedule. I was looking forward to it since two of the classes I had were with Sebastian and Elizabeth. I had forgotten to mention the sexy pajamas situation to Elizabeth. I chose not to mention my birthday plans for Sebastian. It bothered her that I had such a great relationship going and she doesn't get a lot of dates.

Elizabeth and I were getting out of the restroom after retouching our lip-gloss. Sebastian was standing outside. He knew our routine so well. He kissed my lower lip gently. I saw Elizabeth staring and pulled away quickly.

After classes it was finally time for lunch. We went to our usual spot and there was little talk. We were all hungry. I was caressing Sebastian's leg under the table. I couldn't wait to get home that night to be alone with him. He slipped his hand up my wool skirt and rubbed my clit. I was surprised Elizabeth hadn't noticed. I didn't care. I couldn't bring myself to stop him. He knew exactly how to touch me and just then he stopped. He slipped his hand back out. I cleared my throat and took a deep breath. Elizabeth and Sebastian had one more class together. I left for my shift at the store, thinking if lunch was that good, tonight would be amazing.

After work I headed home and immediately got in the shower. As soon as I was finished, the doorbell rang. Sebastian was early. I didn't mind and opened the door. He had this look in his eye, grabbed me and pulled me close. I wrapped my legs around him and the towel fell to the ground as we kissed deep.

He closed the door behind us. He drove me against the wall and his passionate kiss transported me to another world. He held me up with one hand, unbuttoned his pants and slipped his penis inside my warm moistness. Sebastian was thrusting with all his strength. It hurt a little, but I yearned for him.

"Oh yes, baby," I moaned.

Then he grabbed my breast staring lustfully at me. I pushed my head back and closed my eyes. I raked his back with my fingertips. He carried me over to the kitchen sink and started sucking on my clit. I was climaxing as he kept licking. His lips were filled with my juices as he kissed me.

"Ah...Sebastian, ooh!" I screamed when I felt him again inside me. His thrusts were more than I could bear. I held on to the edge of the sink. He closed his eyes and ejaculated inside me.

"Oh Just!" He cried out as he came. I was speechless I was so aroused I wanted him again. I looked at him and he knew. Sebastian scooped my five-foot-eight frame and carried me into the bedroom. We made sexy love all night.

When morning came, I looked over at the clock; we were late. I tapped him. He opened his eyes, saw the time and we both hopped into the shower. Before leaving, he stopped at the door, brushed my curly black hair behind my ears and whispered.

"I love you."

"Ditto," I replied returning his kiss.

Too busy thinking about my baby…

Thursday rolled around quickly. It was Sebastian's birthday and I hoped he would love all I had planned. I spoke to him in the morning and we got through our day. I saw Elizabeth briefly but I still didn't mention my plans for Sebastian's birthday.

There was a box sitting on the bed when he got home. It contained his first gift, a suit for him to wear tonight. I left specific instructions in the box for him. At six, a car would take him to Tavern on the Green Restaurant in Central Park. I was already seated in a tight, black Armai cocktail dress when he arrived.

"Wow baby!" He said beaming with astonishment.

"Happy birthday," I smiled kissing him. He was stunning. The black suit fit him perfectly. He flipped through the menu carefully reading all the entrees. We ordered shrimp cocktail for appetizers and filet mignon.

"This is too much," he said.

"This is only the beginning," I replied with a seductive smile.

Dinner discussion was centered on how we first met and the sweet moments we had shared. Sebastian was taking time to reflect. I loved the look in his eye. It was a combination of appreciation, astonishment and amour all rolled in one.

We finished dinner and moved on to dessert. He had tiramisu and I chose the strawberry cheesecake. When his cake arrived it had a candle in it.

"Make a wish baby," I said.

Later, I fed him the strawberries off the top of my cake. He looked at me like he couldn't wait to get home. When we left the restaurant there was a horse carriage waiting outside.

Sebastian's mouth opened in disbelief. He was speechless and stared blankly at me.

We went for a stroll around the park counting the stars in the sky. He held me so tight and I could feel the love radiating from him. We kissed several times as our ride ended back at the restaurant. We caught a taxi.

"Thank you for making this the best birthday ever," he said.

"You're in for a long night," I replied.

The cab pulled up in front of Dangerfield's. He looked at me and started to laugh already. His favorite comedian was in town. Inside we laughed till our stomachs hurt.

"To Boston," he said raising his glass with gin and tonic. I smiled not understanding why I couldn't share the sentiment. I loved him dearly, but just wasn't a hundred percent sure I was ready to leave.

The show ended and we took a cab to the Copacabana. He was excited. What better way to close the show than to dance the night away inside one of the hottest Latin club.

The curtains came down around four. I was exhausted but had a great time giving this gift. His smile was all the thank-you I needed. Outside, we caught a cab and headed to his place.

As soon as we were in the door, he pushed the strap of my black cocktail dress off my shoulder and started kissing my shoulder gently. Sebastian continued until I was naked and every bit of my body had been touched by his lips. I groaned all morning in pleasure.

Later I left a card on his pillow. I didn't want to wake him. Smiling, I walked out because when he awoke he would read the card.

For all that you are and all that you're not,
I love you, Jus.

Friday was a beautiful, sunny, autumn day. I slipped my heels into new boots from Ralph Lauren. Elizabeth was waiting for me by the classroom door when I got to school.

"Hi sweets, I tried calling you guys last night but no one answered," she said.

"I took Sebastian out for a romantic evening for his birthday. Just the two of us," I replied.

"Oh! I didn't know about that." She said then gave me a blank stare.

"I tried to talk to you about it but you didn't seem too interested," I said.

"That's not true, Justice," she said as we went into the classroom.

That night I went to work at the club but didn't have as much fun as usual. Elizabeth's attitude disturbed me. I felt something was wrong. I kept thinking I'd talk to her tomorrow but that never happened. I never got around to mentioning anything.

Elizabeth called on Sunday and said that she had some papers she needed help with. I told her I would call Sebastian and the two of us would come spend the night. We could do all our papers for Monday. It was a great chance to talk a bit and with Sebastian there, we'd get into all kinds of other discussions. Sebastian met me in the lobby of Elizabeth's dorm.

"Hello," he greeted me with a kiss and we went upstairs. Elizabeth opened the door and her face lit up. It was nothing like the expressions she'd been wearing recently. We walked in and changed into our pajamas. Elizabeth made spaghetti, this time she added garlic bread.

When we were all settled we started writing our papers. Elizabeth needed help with a paper that Sebastian had to do also.

I didn't have that class with them. To make it easier, the two of them sat on the bed and worked on their paper, while I stayed on the makeshift bed to write mine. I finished early.

"What movies do you have?" I asked Elizabeth.

"I don't remember them all sweets, just pick out whatever you like. They're over by the windowsill," she replied.

I headed over to the window and was enthralled by the view. It was raining. I stood staring, thinking of Sebastian and feeling aroused. We weren't alone and I quickly dispatched the thoughts. I looked at all the movie titles. Elizabeth had a large collection. I chose *Threesome*. I hadn't seen it and the title was catching. I popped it in and lowered the volume not to distract them.

"I'm making popcorn, anybody want some?" I asked. Sebastian didn't want any but Elizabeth nodded her head.

Halfway through the movie, my eye lids felt really heavy. I relaxed and closed them. I knew Sebastian would wake me when they were done. I'd sleep next to him. I could still hear the movie.

After some time had passed, I heard what sounded like kissing noises. I thought it was the movie. The sounds intensified and I continued to listen keenly. It had to be a dream. Sebastian and Elizabeth were passionately making out! I wanted to open my eyes but I just couldn't make myself do it. I tried to move my arms, which were crossed over my chest. They wouldn't move. I was screaming at the top of my lungs but no sounds came from my mouth.

A tsunami of pleasure groans enveloped the room. The sound rang clear. They were having sex. My mind wouldn't accept what was going on. I must be having a nightmare thinking I'm awake. Deep down in my heart I knew I wasn't asleep. This was clearly not only true, it was incredible. So many thoughts and images developed in my mind.

All we've been through, for me to be lying two feet away from my boyfriend and my best friend, enveloped in their own fantasies. They were getting down despite me being there. The thought jolted me to reality but I remained immobilized by my emotions.

"Do you think she can hear us?" Elizabeth whispered to Sebastian.

"No," he replied grunting.

I heard the squeak of the mattress as they continued. Completely frozen, I had no control over my body or my thoughts. My tears streamed down landing on the blanket below never making a sound. What had taken years to build was destroyed in a rainy evening's long minute. She moaned through her climax and although she had held it down, I could hear her crying.

Finally they were finished. I stayed frozen like a statue and heard rattling of clothing. It got as quiet as a cemetery after they fell asleep. Hours passed before I could move. I got up quietly and quickly. I grabbed my clothes and got dressed. My mind went completely blank. I stared numbly at them spooning while sleeping.

I had so much to say, it was better to say nothing at all. I did just that. I opened the door right next to where their heads were. The bright light from the dorm hall lit the darkened room awaking them. They both stared at me with the same scared look on their face. I shot each a cold look then slammed the door behind me.

The next several days, I avoided them and school. They called continuously. Sebastian made the mistake of showing up at my house. I didn't answer the door. I couldn't bring myself to do anything but cry. I shed tears for days. The same man that begged me to trust him because he would protect my heart was the same man that destroyed it. I was considering picking up and leaving my life in NY. He never loved me.

I was beside myself in anguish and didn't know what I'd do when I saw them again. The following week I returned to school. I had lost weight from not eating and had bags under my eyes. I looked awful. I had a lot of work to make up. I called my professors and told them I had a death in the family. Luckily, I was an honor student and had never missed class. All my professors agreed to give me an extension.

I walked down the hall and several friends approached me. I played it off not being able to tell anyone what had happened. It was bottled up so well, the only thing I could do now was to heal myself. Finally, I arrived at class where both would be. I sat in the back of the classroom close to the exit. I wanted to make sure I had a quick escape route in case the tears invaded.

They were seated next to each other. Elizabeth turned around when the professor called my name. She passed a note like most students do in high school. I ripped it loud enough for her to hear. I decided exactly what I was going to do. My revenge would be to never allow either of them the opportunity to apologize, or even so much as speak to me.

Class ended and I quickly exited the classroom. By the time they realized, I was already on the train. This continued until the end of the semester. They each tried at different times to approach me or call me. It was like I'd never known them.

I kept to myself, focused on work and used dancing in the clubs as my escape. I always expected Sebastian to walk into the club and had security assigned to me while I was there. He knew it would be to no avail.

Writing poetry became my other form of release. I got sucked in deeper and deeper into the nightlife and rarely came home before six a.m. I started to drink more than usual. I didn't think about them when I was drinking. Sleeping was difficult. I'd be awakened by the sound of her climax.

The semester was slow to the end. I wouldn't have to see their faces anymore. So far, I was successful in making sure they didn't get a chance to speak to me. I changed my phone numbers when I got tired of their attempts at calling to apologize. I scared myself by drinking way too much. Nothing helped. How could it?

Mentally, I went over everything in an attempt to see what had blindsided me. There were things I had noticed but always brushed off. Like his late nights, the sudden change when he'd call or text me. The way Elizabeth had changed.

When she was with Sebastian and me, her face would light up and that defensive, upset look faded. It must have bothered her a lot when I mentioned his birthday and when we kissed in front of her. I wondered how long I was blinded. How long I was the other woman in my own relationship? I was thankful of one thing, he'd never know that I would've said yes. He'd never know how much he meant to me. I'd have moved just to be with him. He'd never know the true secrets of my heart.

Six long years later…

I still close my eyes and the sounds of Elizabeth's moans can fill my head. I was unable to complete college because of financial reasons. Not going back eliminated the possibility of seeing them. I've moved to a fabulous apartment a block from where I used to live. It's new, spacious and fully carpeted one bedroom. I invested so much time into decorating it. I had my friend Edgar driving me continuously to Ikea.

My life has changed except for the fact that I still enjoy a great club or lounge. I'm working at a financial firm and making good salary. I no longer dance at the clubs but go out every chance I get. As time passed I was able to control my drinking. I went on a few dates and realized I couldn't take anyone seriously if I didn't have trust.

I'm living the single life and feeling better in my skin. I've also gotten my spirit back and I'm ready to mingle some.

"What time is it?" Marie asked.

"Its six o'clock," I replied.

Marie was a great co-worker and became a dear friend to me. My relationship with her was very different than what I had with Elizabeth. Marie was tall, skinny and beautiful. She never wore make-up a day in her life; she didn't need to. She was of Black and Philippine decent and had a healthy dark complexion. I enjoyed our talks at work and out. She always seemed genuine in her gestures. Marie became my martini buddy. We had our usual spot and apple martinis with Buffalo wings. Marie and I had just polished off the usual and I decided I wanted to do some dancing.

It was Thursday evening, six p.m. in New York City. You can go dancing anytime of the day, everyday of the week. I decided to go to a place called Jade Terrace. Marie and I caught a cab to get there. Thirty minutes later, we arrived. Traffic was horrendous but we entered the club in good spirits. I knew the night was going to be special. The music was pumping and I was feeling sexy in my maroon cocktail dress. We immediately made our way to the bar.

We had a few more martinis. Before long I'd lost track of Marie. I turned to see her across the room talking with a handsome man. I decided to mingle and help myself to another martini. I was making my way to the bar and heard a familiar voice behind me.

"Jus," the male voice said.

I knew within a second that the voice was none other than Sebastian's. I didn't turn around. I continued walking. I had made it this far and wasn't going to be set back. I had no idea what'd he say. He caught up with me.

"I'm so sorry," he cried out feverishly. "I'm so sorry for what I did to you and to us. I never meant to hurt you and I've been carrying this around for so many years. Justice, it's killing me," he said.

I didn't turn around. Other club-goers noticed us. His voice was raised. Finally, I looked back at him. I could tell he meant every word he'd just said. He was wearing a black suit with gray shirt and had a fresh haircut. He seemed to be doing well for himself. I wasn't about to ask.

"Do you feel better?" I asked.

"Yes," He answered sternly.

"Good because I don't!"

I turned around and walked away. I saw the pain in his eyes. We had a beautiful relationship and greed destroyed it. He'd have to live with that for the rest of his life. I continued walking and couldn't help but smile. It had taken six years but I knew my reaction to what happened that night was the right one. There was no punishment worse than the weight of your own guilt.

There were lessons learned that dreadful day. Most importantly not to bring your man around your female friends in such a relaxed environment like Elizabeth and me shared. You can't help if two people are attracted to each other. They'll do whatever they please.

We as woman need not provide any tools or make it easier either. No matter how many times I would have thought to slap each of them in the face, I wouldn't have felt as happy as I do right now. I never saw Elizabeth again. She'll carry that weight around forever. Sebastian got to say he was sorry. I now had Justice and a book filled with poetic memories.

Mended

I shall learn

It was not I,

I shall be fond

Of my innocence

I will settle down

And lower my voice

Though-

It made a sound to no one at all

The cries

As I sat up all night

I would learn to love

To trust and appreciate

Once more

Walls adjusted,

But yes

Once more!

I'm taking with me the strength of the fight

I'm taking it all with me

I learned,

I learned

How to save my life!

Dedicated to Fallon Brown, your honesty and continuous encouragement has contributed greatly to my inspirations...

unfinished business

Leah Whitney

Simone stared at Todd in shock as her fiancé, Chris, reached into his wallet to pay for the gas he had just pumped into his brand new powder blue Lexus. Todd had been working at the station for three months now, and he suddenly seemed to be aware of his shabby appearance. He hadn't slept a full night in weeks, and he looked slightly older than his twenty-seven years.

"Fine, ain't she?" Chris said to Todd as he and Simone cruised out of the gas station onto Merrick Road toward their beautiful Long Island home. Todd, still holding the gas pump, nodded awkwardly in agreement, while Simone lowered her head and began fidgeting with the car radio tuner. It had been more than a year since they last laid eyes on one another, and the strange feeling now in the pit of Todd's stomach and the questioning look in Simone's eyes said it all: They definitely had some unfinished business to settle.

"You know you look good, right, baby?" Chris said massaging Simone's thigh as they merged onto the Southern State Parkway.

"Sure," she replied flatly. *Now he decides to give me a half-ass compliment after ignoring me all day,* she thought. Normally she'd be more irritated at his lack of attentiveness, but her mind was on Todd now. Seeing him again was beginning to make her feel overwhelmed with sadness.

Simone blinked back the tears and looked straight ahead as Chris picked up speed and switched lanes. "Turn that up for me, hon," he said, bopping his head to the steady beat pumping from his custom-made speakers in the roof of the car.

Todd pulled into his driveway and parked his black Chevy Tahoe. He leaned his six-foot-one-inch, dark chocolate physique back in the driver's seat and let out a heavy sigh. He hadn't stopped thinking about Simone since seeing her hours earlier. On the way home, he had made a detour and went to the neighborhood bar for a few drinks; he wanted to numb his thoughts, but that hadn't worked. Simone was still heavy on his mind.

Todd ambled up the cement steps and stuck his key in the door of the top floor apartment he rented in a two-family house in Queens. He pushed open the door and started to unbutton his dingy grey shirt. He tossed his boots and the rest of his clothing, and then jumped into the shower.

Todd stood under the showerhead and let the hot water stream over his bald head and down his muscular back. Memories of taking showers with Simone suddenly came rushing to him, and he thought about the last time they were together.

He remembered her perfectly toned arms and legs tightly wrapped around him. Kisses were passionate and strokes were deep. Simone sweetly moaned and called out his name until her body shook with ecstasy. He pleased her again and again until she could take no more.

I better stop thinking about her, Todd thought while lathering his six-pack. But after only a few seconds he began daydreaming about Simone's caramel colored skin. Thoughts of her long, jet-black hair and almond-shaped brown eyes frustrated him, not to mention the fact that there was a new man in her life now, and she looked well taken care of. But Simone always took good care of herself and still looked a lot younger than her actual age. She was nine years older than Todd, but she didn't look a day over twenty-five.

Todd grabbed a towel from the hook on the bathroom door and wrapped it around his waist. He walked into the kitchen and got a beer before going to the living room to turn on the TV. He plopped down heavily on the couch and picked up the remote.

Todd lay back as he began to feel the tension leave his body. He tried to fight fatigue, flicking the same digital channels back and forth without paying attention to what was on the screen. Finally, he fell into a restless slumber with the remote still in his hand—and Simone still on his brain.

"Ooh, Simone...ooh, yeah, baby..." Chris moaned as he quickly thrust his semi-erect penis in and out of her. The only time Simone got a glimpse of his emotions was when they had sex, which was never a big deal and always left her empty. She was really in no mood tonight, especially after he had treated her like a trophy piece earlier at his friend Steven's backyard cookout.

Chris was constantly trying to impress his friends. He always pretended that he and Simone were the perfect, happy pair. That was far from the truth. Simone and Chris hardly spoke about anything these days that didn't pertain to his future plans at the real estate firm where he worked, but whenever they went out in public he laid it on thick, like they were the happiest couple in the universe. Simone would see red. The only reason she hadn't rocked the boat yet was because her parents adored him. Her mother always made sure to remind her of how lucky she was to have a man—especially a black man—who was doing so well. "Girl, how many more black men do you think you're gonna find like Chris? Ya betta hold onto him. If I was just ten years younger, your father would have something to worry about. Don't you mess up things with that man," she'd always say.

Chris gripped Simone's buttocks as he prepared to relieve himself. Simone was numb, but she moved her body along with his to get it over with. Chris didn't have a whole lot of stamina like Todd, and she was so glad for that. Being with Chris was getting to be too much of a chore lately, and she now wished she hadn't given him her number a year ago.

It was a Sunday morning, and Simone was doing her usual jog around the track when she noticed Chris running alongside her. She immediately became annoyed; she didn't like being distracted when she ran. When Chris told her that the only way he would leave her alone was if she gave him her phone number, she didn't hesitate to give up the digits. It was the only way to get rid of him.

Things began to move quickly after their first few dates. After just three months, Chris asked Simone to move in with him. She did, and before long they were engaged. However, Simone didn't feel fully at peace about her decision to marry him. It wasn't that she didn't find him attractive. Chris was a brown-skinned, well toned, six-footer with hazel eyes. He always smelled good and dressed well. He was educated and definitely a keeper—on the surface—but his selfishness and arrogance became too much to bear as the months rolled by.

Chris could also be a real dick at times, but everyone seemed to go along with it because he had money. Simone, too, had gone along with it in the beginning, but only because she was confused and hurt after Todd had stopped calling and eventually disappeared from her life altogether. She was on the rebound. She finally admitted it now. Simone had been lying to herself all along about being in love with Chris. Todd was her true love, and here she was caught up with a man she didn't even like.

"Hey, baby, I'm talking to you. Put you in a trance, huh?" Chris said repeating himself as he walked out of the adjacent bathroom wearing nothing but a pair of house slippers. He approached the king-sized bed where Simone lay between the off-white sheets. He stood looking down at her now.

"Huh?" Simone remained numb. She lay flat on her back looking up at the ceiling. The blank expression on her face wasn't one of a woman who'd just had fulfilling sex. But Chris didn't even consider that possibility for a second. "Oh... yeah, you do it every time. You know that," Simone said. Chris now wore a cocksure grin. Nobody could tell him he wasn't the shit—nobody.

Simone woke up early the next morning. She tiptoed with her duffel bag to the bathroom so as not to wake Chris, who usually slept like a log.

She scrubbed her five-foot-seven-inch frame with a

soapy loofah as if trying to rid herself of something dirty. Then she rubbed her skin hard with an open hand as the water from the showerhead beat down on it. She started to grab the soap again, but decided against it. She needed to get going.

Simone quickly got dressed in a white T-shirt and stretch blue jeans. She checked her sleek ponytail in the mirror and applied a little lip gloss. She took a deep sigh and threw her bag over her shoulder, only to find Chris standing before her when she opened the bathroom door, yawning and running his hand across his thick, closely cropped hair. *Just my luck,* she thought.

"Hey, where you goin'?" Chris asked groggily.

"Uh…jogging, like I do every Sunday—remember?" Simone lied. She never showered before jogging.

"Oh, yeah. Well, have fun," Chris said nonchalantly before turning to go downstairs to the kitchen. He worked out regularly himself, but only at the gym with his colleagues, just to be in the loop about any new business developments. Working out with Simone was one of the last things he'd ever do. There was no payoff.

Simone felt relieved as she slowly backed out of the driveway. She glanced at the sprawling front lawn of the home she shared with Chris. It meant nothing to her. The only time she felt totally at peace lately was when she was in her bright red Honda Accord. It was her sanctuary.

Simone heard her favorite slow jam on the radio when she turned the corner. It immediately sparked memories of Todd. How he had admired her with his sexy brown eyes. The butterflies in her stomach confirmed her decision: She had to go and see him.

Simone pulled up to the gas station. The pumps were unattended and Todd was nowhere in sight. Simone parked and waited. Soon an attendant showed up and asked her if she needed help.

"I'm looking for...uh...Todd Michaels," Simone said nervously.

"He don't work on Sundays," said the stocky attendant, leaning into the driver's side window of the Honda.

Simone paused for a moment. "Okay, well...can you please give this to him for me?" she said after reaching into her bag and retrieving a pen and a torn piece of paper. She handed him the paper with her name and cell number written on it.

"Well, he's not here and I am..."

"Thank you," Simone said ending any possible

conversation with him before pulling off.

"That's a fine-ass piece," the attendant said under his breath as he watched the Honda disappear down the street.

Derek had barely gotten into his apartment good before grabbing the phone to call Todd. "Yo, man, some fine-ass chick drove into the station today looking for you," he said into the receiver as he flopped down onto a loud, print-patterned couch. "Why you ain't tell me you was gettin' the honeys like that? Anyway, T, I told her you don't work on Sundays, and she left her name and number."

Todd was driving home from his mother's house in Brooklyn. He was exhausted after laying new tiles in her kitchen, and he wasn't up for any idle chitchat, much less Derek's bullshit. Was he talking about Simone? Todd wondered, thinking back to how awkward the few moments they shared staring at one another felt.

"What was the name?" he asked impatiently, while turning off the radio as he exited the Belt Parkway.

"Simone, her name is Simone. Ask her do she got a friend for me, man. Maybe we could all double-date or somethin'."

"How about giving me the number first, Derek?"

Derek read off the number and continued to run his mouth. "You know you owe me, right, slick?" I mean, I don't usually—"

Todd pressed the button on his cell phone, ending Derek's rambling. There was no need for him to write down Simone's number; it was still the same and he knew it by heart. He pulled into his driveway, hoping nothing else had changed. He hopped out of his ride and strolled into his apartment, humming his favorite love song.

Simone sat in her office at the design firm where she worked. She examined a few sketches on her desk of velour jogging suits that were scheduled for upcoming release. It was lunchtime, and she could have been out enjoying the warm summer air.

"Girl, don't tell me you're still in that same position looking at those same sketches. Come on out with me and help me pick out some shoes for this jam I'm going to this weekend."

Simone looked up and saw her best friend and co-worker, Davina. They had both joined the company three years ago and worked their way up to marketing executive positions. Davina made her job look effortless, while Simone seemed to always be pondering her next decision.

"Go without me, okay? I gotta decide on which logo works best for this new line," Simone said. The frown she wore said more.

"He still hasn't called you, huh, sweetie?" Davina said realizing that Simone had other things on her mind besides work.

"Unh-uh. Who was I kidding? I'd just rolled up with Chris," Simone said returning to the sketches, not wanting Davina to see her eyes water. It was too late.

"Don't worry. He'll call. It's only been a little over—" Davina changed the subject. "Look, girl, I basically know which shoes I want, so I'll just go and grab the sandwich in my drawer and come back here. We'll have lunch in your office, all right?"

"Davina, go and get your shoes. I'm okay."

"But Simone, you shouldn't be—"

"Go...just go," Simone said a little too harshly. She didn't mean to, but it came out that way. She didn't want to talk about Todd after the way he'd left her hanging. Truth be told, she was livid. The idea of spending her life with Chris didn't seem so bad after all.

Six weeks had passed, and Simone couldn't believe how well she and Chris had been getting along. He was turning out to be everything she always wanted in a man. He had become less obnoxious and arrogant, and he was a whole lot more attentive to her needs. She could work with that.

On a few occasions when Simone had thought about picking up the phone and calling Todd, she thought about how Chris had practically done a three-sixty. She felt guilty and decided against contacting Todd, even though she was really curious about how he wound up working at a gas station; she remembered him landing a good job at a bank downtown.

"Would you like something from inside, baby? I need to take this call in the house," Chris said to Simone before picking up his ringing cell phone. They'd each taken the day off from work to spend some time together, and they'd been lounging all morning by the pool in their spacious backyard.

"No, sweetie, I'm fine. Handle your business," Simone confidently replied, shifting her body in the cozy lounge chair.

She was sure it was a call from his office, and she didn't want him to miss out on any important deals.

Simone watched Chris as he walked up the patio steps and pressed the button that opened and closed the sliding glass door. She closed her eyes to take a catnap as he turned on the stereo inside the house. Her favorite slow jam began playing again. She tried to ignore it, but it got louder. Simone leaned forward, covering her ears from the sound of piano keys and saxophone cutting through the peaceful afternoon air. It was still too loud. She fought to keep the memories of Todd from creeping back up on her. It was no use. She could no longer just sit there.

Why does Chris have that music turned up so loud? she thought pressing the button to open the patio door. *What's up with him all of a sudden?*

Simone walked to the stereo in the living room and searched for the off switch.

"I can never find a damn thing on this contraption," she muttered under her breath with her hands on her hips.

Simone found the control panel a few seconds later and lowered the music after changing the station. Satisfied with Mary J. Blige, she turned to walk back outside, but she stopped dead in her tracks when she heard Chris loud and clear in the kitchen, still on the phone.

"I could've stayed fucking that other bitch, but you know, she wasn't marriage material. Simone will help me get to that next level, even though she is a dry fuck most of the time," Chris said with a chuckle.

Simone stood frozen. She couldn't believe what she had just heard. That couldn't have been Chris. That was just someone impersonating him. Yeah, that was it. She took a step toward the sliding glass door when she heard him again.

"Yeah, I'm only marrying her ass for appearances. It looks good for a brotha to have a sista like her on his arm in the business world. I'm about to do big things, and I'll be turning the big 4-0 in a couple of years. Having a chick like Simone definitely won't hurt nothin', especially when I make partner."

Simone almost forgot where she was, much less why she had even come into the house. She began to shake involuntarily. Chris continued. "Yeah, she was acting a little strange there a few weeks ago, but I put it on her and now she's all in one hundred percent again. I figure I'll marry her just in time for the company Christmas party this year. But she don't know about that yet. That's why I've been acting extra sweet lately. She won't even entertain the thought of waiting to marry me. But to tell you the truth…humph…I'm the best thing that ever happened to that frigid bitch. She's lucky to have me."

Chris ended his call and walked out of the kitchen and through the living room toward the patio. He could have sworn he closed the patio door when he came inside, but then again, maybe not. He pressed the button to close the door behind him and looked out by the pool to find Simone fast asleep. Life with her would be a cinch.

"Hey, gorgeous, you sleep?" Chris whispered in Simone's ear.

Simone played it cool. With her eyes still closed, she shifted around in the lounge chair, pretending to be getting in a more comfortable position. After a few moments, she opened her eyes and saw Chris lying in the chair beside her.

Todd motioned for the old woman to pull up closer to the pump. It was the middle of a hot afternoon and the last place he wanted to be was at work, inhaling exhaust pipe fumes all day. He gave the woman her change and picked the pump back up to service the next vehicle.

After being laid off from the bank, Todd worked several odd jobs in addition to putting in twelve-hour shifts at the gas station. He really hated pumping gas now, especially after seeing Simone. Even if she *was* sick of ol' boy pushing the Lex, he was nowhere near ready for her. She was definitely high maintenance. It hurt his pride to admit that, but he had to protect himself from any possible embarrassment. It was best that he didn't call her.

"Did you call brown sugar yet?" Derek asked him. Ignoring the blank look on Todd's face, he proceeded. "Man, you crazy. That chick's fine. And she's feelin' you, too? I bet if she wanted *me* to call her, I'd be all over that ass. Keep sleepin'," he added before motioning to the driver of the approaching van to pull up to the pump on the other side.

Todd understood where Derek was coming from, but knew there was nothing he could do right now. The last thing a girl like Simone wanted was a guy who pumped gas for a living. He'd almost summoned enough courage to call her once or twice, but the more he thought about his current financial situation, the more inadequate he felt.

"You all right, babe?" Chris asked rubbing Simone's thigh.

"Better than ever, now that you're here," she said trying to sound normal. All the time she had spent feeling guilty over the past several weeks, thinking she was fooling him, only to find out he'd been scheming on her since day one.

"Sure you don't want me to get you anything—anything at all?" Chris asked.

"No…well…yeah, there *is* something you can get." She wanted to scream at the top of her lungs, but she braced herself instead. She'd have a trick for his ass soon enough, but there'd be enough time for that later.

"Okay, tell me. What is it?" Chris said. "How about some Chinese food? I have a real taste fo some shrimp fried rice. Can you go get that for me?"

Chris was a little surprised. That was the last thing he expected to hear. Simone had seemed to enjoy being up under him over the past few weeks, and he didn't think she'd be sending him on an errand for food when there was so much of it in the house.

Chris hopped in his car after Simone added Utz barbecue potato chips and Swedish candy fish to her order. He'd have to go to three different stores to get everything she wanted. That was just fine with him. He wasn't about to screw shit up at this point; there was too much at stake.

Simone waved to Chris as he backed out of the driveway. When he was out of sight, she picked up her cell phone to call her mother. There was no doubt in her mind that she would tell her to pack her bags.

"Well, stop being a dry fuck then," Mrs. Taylor said nonchalantly after Simone had given her a word-for-word account of everything she had heard during Chris' phone conversation. "And with all that running and stretching and knowing so much about your body like you do, it seems you'd be more creative. I don't underst—"

Click. Simone snapped her phone shut. Once again, her mother had successfully managed to make it to the very top of her shit list. She could be downright unbelievable at times.

Simone went upstairs to the bedroom, laid across the bed and cried hysterically. In order to appear calm when Chris returned, she had to let it all out.

She began the breathing exercises she had recently learned in a yoga class. A few minutes later, she was back in control. *I'll show him who's a dry fuck,* she thought, sashaying down the winding staircase that led back to the main floor.

Chris returned with the food and sweets to a perfectly set kitchen table. Simone really did have an appetite now, and her mouth watered when the aroma of the freshly cooked food hit her nostrils. Chris had also bought a quart of sweet and sour chicken for himself, and they split the food and ate heartily.

"Know what I'm thinking?" Simone asked playfully, watching Chris swallow his last bit of fried rice.

"Oh, not now, hon. I haven't even digested my food."

"I'm not talking about now!" Simone said laughing. "Hell, I'm not even talking about later on tonight."

Chris looked puzzled. He definitely wanted to get his hump on later, regardless.

"What are you talking about?" he said anxiously.

"You're such a good lover, Chris," Simone lied. "I want to really show you how much I appreciate you. Sometimes I feel like you deserve so much more than I'm giving you...if you know what I mean."

"Uh huh," Chris said poking out his chest. Maybe he wouldn't have to get with that new little temp at the office after all—at least not right away. His imagination was stirred, and he smiled.

"I'd like to do something really special for you,"

Simone added

"Okay, keep going," Chris said, his arrogance barely hidden now.

"It's a surprise." Simone was beaming, and Chris couldn't wait to find out what she had in store for him.

"Give me a hint," he said inquisitively.

"I can't, but I *will* tell you that you're going to be one happy man this Friday night."

Simone got off early on Fridays, so everything would fall right into place. Chris was satisfied with the two-day wait. He'd rush home right after work on Friday so Simone could serve him like the king he was. It was about time she learned how to come correct and handle her business. He was sure he'd need to guide her along, though. But it was high time she proved herself worthy of the dick.

⋘◉⋙

Chris put his key in the door and swaggered into the house with high expectations. Simone had given him simple directions to follow: He'd take a shower and then lie naked on the bed on his stomach and wait for her. He'd wear the blindfold that was left under the pillow.

Chris quickly showered and dried himself off. Looking

around, there was no Simone to be found. He knew she'd appear shortly. She was hungry for him and had every reason to be.

Music from Sade's *Love Deluxe* hummed in the background. Chris smiled as he imagined himself giving it up to Simone with no mercy. Lying naked on the bed, he adjusted the blindfold. He soon felt the light touch of fingers moving gently across his back. His skin tingled. *A subtle start,* he thought to himself. Chris relaxed when a moist tongue began licking the back of his thighs and butt cheeks, making him squirm.

"Oh, Simone," he moaned.

Chris was totally surprised at Simone's newfound creativity. The thought that this could be a three-way was beginning to turn him on.

Soft hands bound his wrists together while another pair applied light massage. Certain now that this was a three-way, his manhood stirred. He twisted his torso in an effort to turn over. He was pushed back onto his stomach. "Oh, feeling a little aggressive this evening, huh, girls?" Seconds later his butt cheeks were spread open. "What the fuck is up, Simone?"

"Hold on, playa. If you don't fight it, you won't get hurt," a deep, masculine voice stated.

"Whoa! Who the fuck are *you*?" Chris asked beginning

to struggle.

You remember Rodney. I'm Simone's gay first cousin. We met way back when you weren't fuckin' up.

"Whatcha doin'?" Chris' stomach was churning now.

"Well, Simone asked me to help her settle a score. When I heard it was with you, why, I told her I'd be more than happy to oblige. The idea of you getting it like you is, well, that was mine, Chrissie baby."

"C'mon, you've got to be—"

Chris kicked his feet wildly when he felt Rodney's hardness up against his ass.

"You don't even wanna know how often I've secretly fantasized about having my way with your sweet ass," Rodney whispered in Chris' ear.

"Yo, get the fuck off me! This some bullshit, man! I ain't fuckin' gay! Huh…? Ugh…ah-h-h!" Chris could no longer speak when he felt the sharp pain from the pressure on his anus. Rodney's rock hard dick was entering him slowly but surely.

"Didn't I tell you not to fight it?" he said tightening the blindfold. "You're about to make things a lot harder on yourself," he added nonchalantly. Rodney hefted the full weight of his muscular body on Chris and licked his earlobe.

Then, without further hesitation, he repeatedly rammed his cock into him until the skin around his asshole tore and bled. Chris trembled and shook.

"Please don't do this shit, man! I'm begging you!" he screamed in agony. There was no escape. Rodney's six-foot-five-inch, two hundred and forty-pound frame proved to be too much to handle.

"Oh, y-e-e-e-a-a-h! Christmas done came early; I done caught me a virgin!" Rodney sang, his nine-inch cock now fully inside Chris' anal cavity. He thrust and thrust until Chris had used up all of his energy and could no longer fight.

"Now, see…doesn't that feel better? Big daddy ain't gon' hurt you." Rodney's strokes were gentle now. He was in his glory, almost forgetting that he had taken Chris against his will, until he quickly glanced at his tightly bound wrists.

"Hmm…ah…?" Chris moaned. He was limp, defeated, his manhood snatched from him. He gathered his thoughts as Rodney continued to stroke him. The conclusion was overwhelming: Simone had set him up lovely.

Rodney put an unloaded gun to the back of Chris' head. "I could kill your bitch ass for fucking wit' my fam! Do you realize that?" he growled.

"Yes, yes!" Chris cried out.

"But damn, because you're a good lay, I'ma let you live!"

Rodney pounded into Chris with more vigor now, smacking his ass cheeks as a camera flash went off from the side of the bed. *Women can be so helpful,* he thought.

After taking care of business, Rodney pulled off in his car from where he had parked it around the corner.

Simone's cell phone rang. Seeing Rodney's name on the caller ID, she picked it up.

"Hey, what's up? Okay, so what did you do? All right…" Simone was a little disappointed. Rodney wasn't giving her the complete lowdown, and she truly wanted to know what the deal was. She probed again. "Rodney, what did you d—?"

Rodney had already snapped his phone shut. Simone knew her cousin was raw when it came to revenge. Hell, that's why she had called him in the first place, but she would never know how raw he really was.

Sunday quickly came around again, and Simone already completed her first lap around the track. It had been a month since she had moved all of her things out of the house after getting off from work early that Friday. She hadn't heard from Chris since, and she was now staying with Davina temporarily. She had expected Chris to at least call and cuss her out, but when she hadn't heard a peep out of him she decided to accept the shitty way things had ended between them as closure.

Simone was sure now that whatever Rodney had done, he did it to the fullest. She didn't believe the cockamamie story he had finally told her one bit. She placed the sole of her sneaker on the edge of the bench and stretched.

A tall, handsome figure approached from across the track. *It can't be,* she thought. Davina had acted funny the other day when Simone told her she didn't care if she never saw him again. She must've told him where to find her.

"Hello, beautiful," Todd said standing before her. Simone was speechless, but the look in his eyes said it all: He had come to settle their unfinished business.

sweet 306
Tri Smith

A short story from
"The Bristol Ho-tel. Wicked...Twisted...Sex."

Audruana sat naked on the lid of the toilet with her elbows on her thighs. Her dangling hands held two tiny triangles of transparent pink fabric, just scraps.

Sweet had handed them to her after hastily rummaging through a cardboard box filled with flimsies sitting outside the bathroom door. Edged in skimpy pink marabou feathers, satin strings connected the two wee pieces that made the top. The bottom was the merest thong with a front patch that couldn't fully cover a crotch, anybody's.

She was supposed to put them on and dance. Audition, in

the bedroom right outside the closed bathroom door, from music off the radio. In front of Sweet 306 was the extravagant hustler she'd met a few hours earlier at the bar on Broadway and 51st, The Mozambique. Her silver vinyl cat suit was in a heap atop strapped, rhinestone stilettos on top of that was her silver thong.

Sweet 306 told her he was an adult entertainment producer and booking agent when he'd introduced himself at the bar. Conversation revealed that Audruana liked to dance. After lavish compliments on her pretty face and sexy figure, she'd been persuaded to leave with him in a cab, then to stop at his place and show him a few of her moves. He was looking for fresh talent.

"Strictly biz," he promised.

"Okay," Audruana agreed to go with him. How else could he hire her if he didn't know what she could do?

Sweet 306 informed her he was a busy man. It was unusual that he even had this time tonight. She had to come with him now, right now. Tomorrow was out of the question, he'd be leaving town.

He had an immediate spot open for a dancer at a fabulous high-class club that he did business with on Long Island. Whoever he hired for the job had to be exceptional because this club was premium, top flight. Only the best-built, most beautiful talented girls would be considered for the hot stage, the money was long. He'd interviewed a few amazing girls already this week. He needed another Black girl.

Sweet confessed in the back of the taxi on their very short ride to his suite that he thought he'd already made up his mind on who he'd hire. Her name was Passion. She was a rich brown African-Hawaiian, natural wonder with big tits and straight black hair down to her big, round ass. That all changed when he saw Audruana at the bar. She was shining like a star.

Sweet 306 stayed in Suite 306. It wasn't a suite at all, but a hotel room, built like a small box and a turn around bathroom with just a sink, narrow shower and a toilet. The room was at the Bristol Hotel, midtown, on 48th Street, between 8th and 9th Avenues.

Through the bathroom door, she heard him let someone into the room.

She listened and caught his greeting.

"What's up boss-man?"

She heard no response.

Why did she lie to Sweet? She told him she was a professional dancer. She had been a principal rump-shaker in a few videos, choreographed a few more and worked in a couple of bars swinging on poles.

She was counting on how she looked. Audruana Hillton stood up and tied the halter strings around her neck. She reached around her back to make a bow with two more. The top was so small, it swelled her breast out the sides and they kissed like lovers in the center. She stepped into the thong and the back string disappeared deep into her crotch. Unsuccessfully, she tried pushing underneath the tiny front sheerness and all the soft brown hair that escaped. Audruana looked down pulling at a few of the insouciant strands curling at the tops of her thighs; she was so damn bushy.

"Sekshul!" That's how he said the name he gave her an hour ago. "Sekshul! What's up baby? Whutchu doin in there? Put that thang on an' come on out."

"Hold on a minute! I'll be right out!"

Sexual pretended a few dance stretches then swept her arms overhead in a grand final pose. She opened the bathroom door and came out barefooted.

"See? Whut I say! She built like she stepped from yo dreams an' shit! An' all her beauty is natchul an' shit!"

Sweet leaned over and nudged his partner.

Propped against the queen size headboard was Sweet 306

and his partner lounged on the flocked red bedspread. Sweet's partner had on a white Stetson with a broad brim broken to hide his eyes. A strong copper brown nose sat proudly over a perfect thick black mustache that turned into two expertly clipped lines leading down to a thick black goatee. Both of his full lips were turned down. A strip of red showed inside the bottom one.

He wore a black silk shirt, black leather pants and a black leather vest. All around the vest, the collar of the shirt and down the sides of the pants were stitched in white. A diamond nearly the size of a dime sparkled from one ear. Around his neck from a platinum chain; "Joker" hung in diamond script, including the quotations. He didn't wear any other jewelry. Thin black silk socks covered his long feet. He held a smoldering joint in one hand and the other a full glass of amber liquid. A large cobalt ashtray marked the space between him and Sweet.

"It's about damn time! Shit!" Sweet blasted baritone bellowed. Then softening his voice he added. "Whutchu was doin' in there so long? I ain't used to waitin', baby." Sweet's short thick legs stretched at full length and stopped halfway the bed. Audruana saw he'd changed out of his eggplant silk suit.

He wore a purple silk lounging robe that slid from his fat, round shoulders whenever he moved the slightest, revealing his creased nudity. His Buddha belly rested comfortably atop his soft banana thighs. Covered in tangled black hair his breasts hung like teats. The heavy gold chain of a gold and diamond medallion molded like the map of Africa was caught in his cleavage.

Most of his sausage fingers were rigid with large diamond rings. Sweet's flashy gold and diamond watch sucked one wrist. A wide gold bracelet studded with diamonds circled the other. His stubby toes looked like they could be popped off his round feet like big pale grapes. His long toenails were shiny with clear polish.

Latin in his background gave his head a crop of curly black hair, but Father Time and his mama's genes had already started to take it off on the top.

Sweet's cheeks, his jaw line and chin were fat from overindulgence. He loved to eat. His body showed the thick broiled steaks rimmed with a fine inch of fat, cornmeal-fried porgies, his favorite double-cut apple-stuffed pork chops, stewed potatoes homemade cake, red rice and beans.

"Go 'head Sekshul, turn to sump'n on the radio an' groove me, sugar. Whutchu say to me when I metchu tonight? Huh! You said you like mekin' money, right? Huh, baby? Didn'chu say that?"

He reached into the ashtray and picked up an etched glass vial topped with a silver cap. Sweet twisted it off then lifted a tiny silver spoon from the ashtray and dipped it in the full container. Two hits traveled through each nostril. He dug the spoon in one more time and sprinkled powder on his tongue. It ran quickly across his gums. Powerfully, he sniffed a few times then sneezed with might.

Sweet cleared his throat.

"If you serious 'bout getting' paid, I can schedule you right away. Whutchu think baby? All you got to do is dance and pocket three, fo' hunnit a night! Easy! An' I'm a still get mine. Yeah!"

Sweet's plump finger glittered as he pinched his nostrils together and massaged them. He let go and chuckled.

"An' that's the dough you gon' clock from the jump, jus' cause you would be the new girl. You gon' double it. I'm a say in a munt once muhfuckas know a boss broad like you is rump-shakin'. Knowhumsayin' baybay? You ready to get paid? Ready to rake the money you make, not fake the money you make? Huh, honey? Knowhumsayin'? Yeah!"

Sexual ran the dial up and down the radio, not pausing at any frequency long enough to hear the rhythm of a song. Numbers changed rapidly on the display. She was thinking. She wanted the deep green Sweet was promising in her pocket. She just had to gloss through this audition well enough to get over. She could change the rules once she got hip to how the game ran.

"Come on! Stop bullshittin! Wastin' my muthafuckin' time! Pick sump'n an' dance!"

Sweet had that hard voice again. Sexual let the radio stay on 'BLS, an oldie, Stevie Wonder's, *Higher Ground* had just gotten started.

Standing motionless, she began a sway that soon became creative, interpretive movements. The only space to perform was a rectangular piece of red carpet between the foot of the bed and the dresser. She didn't put her eyes on the men. She acted out the phrases of the song with a dancer's see something far-away gaze. Sexual kicked her leg high, let it find the floor in a lunge, her arms fluttered like wind banners. She rose slowly to her toes turned some spins and dropped to a crouch, following her nose around in circles.

Because she wasn't watching him Audruana didn't see Joker slide off the bed. As she was about to leap he caught her by her shoulder and walked her backwards until her back was flush against the wall beside the dresser. His grip stayed tight until she understood that he wanted her to be still.

Breathing audibly, Audruana looked from Joker to Sweet then back again. What was wrong? She was scared to ask.

"You said you could dance, Sek-shul! What the fuck was that shit? I know ain't nobody paid yo' ass to do no bullshit like that. Jerkin' aroun' like you havin' a muthafuckin' fit an' shit! You gotta be kiddin'."

Sweet sniffed more cocaine up his nose.

Joker took his hands off Sexual and got back into his spot on the bed. James Brown stated belting *Sex Machine*.

"Ah yeah! Aw shit! They gon' back in the day! I ain't heard this shit in a while! Turn that shit up! Now dance baby! Aw shucks, James is my muthafucka!"

Stay on the scene…like a sex machine…

"This my shit!"

Sweet had the bed bouncing and the springs complaining. Silent Joker rode the moving bed unconcerned, doing blow.

"Come on, baby! Move yo' big pretty ass! Groove to the music, Sekshul! Whip them big hips. Bounce them titties!"

Sweet took a big swig from his Hennessy.

"Aw yeah, I feel like partying now! Come on, baby, dance fo' Sweet an' make me want to take sump'n you got. Make me hard. You want this job? Dance for cash, Sekshul, shake that ass!"

Audruana moved off the wall yanking off her top, popping the strings. Her beautiful large breasts bounced, free swaying on their own. She stepped quickly to the bed snatched Sweet's glass and threw the amber down her throat. She drank it so greedily and quickly a small amount trickled over her chin, down her throat between her tits to leave its last dribble in the well of her navel.

She took the spliff in Joker's hand, put it between her lips and steamed it, pulling heavy drags of smoke into her lungs. All the while she was twisting, letting James' funk put a grind in her hips that got deeper with every revolution.

Sexual wanted to work for Sweet 306. She just had to get her head bad to do what she had to do. She shimmied over to the dresser and strangled the liquor bottle by its neck, threw away the top and gulped. The healthy stream of cognac, burning her throat.

She rolled her hips back to the bed, jumped on it on her knees, her globes jiggling luscious and ripe. She stole the fat joint from the ashtray and hit it hard again. She leaned into Joker and accepted the blow he fed up her nose. James' squeals spun through the room. The weed, liquor and cocaine rode the music and collided inside her head. Audruana 's head was torn up. She was ready to be anything that Sweet wanted.

She pushed off the bed and stood sideways to the men. She put her palms on her wide bent knees and began thrusting her pelvis back and forth in time to the music, humping hard, head hanging down like she couldn't help her nasty self.

She acted like there were strong masculine hands holding her waist, keeping her from escaping the savage pumping he was delivering from behind. Audruana bucked like her transparent slayer had his knees bent too, getting up under it to get it good. Stroking in the most selfish get-all-this-poom-poom way.

She slid her palms down the front of her legs to shimmy her big behind, shivering and taunting, craving more. He-who-wasn't-there straightened his muscular legs and slid in his see through steel again. His bang was strong. Sexual bent her knees not to fall. Her quivering pretended that the-porn-star-ghost was steady grinding, socking inside too good to pull out.

Sexual swung her ass around and faced the men. Her succulent breasts were heaving, long legs spread and arms hanging limply from her sides. She kept her head down. She was breathless, sucking air in gasps as if a nasty lover had sneaked between her legs at that very moment to thoroughly use his lips as a favor to her burning desire.

Her hands touched her own flat belly wonderingly again, like she was being mauled by some man's hands, fingers splayed, groping, delighted, discovering the lushness of her large breasts.

She let her head loll as her fingers roamed, greedily kneading their heavy softness. She jiggled them and bounced them on her palms and pressed them together hard, like a wish for something thick slipping between her canyon.

She aroused her jutting nipples even further, pinching and rolling them hard to the point of pain that was good. Pulsing needles of lust turned into glistening patches of nectar wetting the inside of her thighs.

She took her self-pleasuring down to the floor till on her hands and knees, Sexual glanced over her shoulder at the two rabid men in the room.

"Goodman! Look how wet you is, girl! Ye-e-e-ah bay-bay, thas whut I talkin' bout. Go head bay-bay! Get off! Whus up? Can you take more than one at a time? You's double-dip freak! Sho you right, bay-bay. Ssss-aahhh, I wasn' gon' take none but you got me changin' my muhfuckin mind."

Sweet looked over at Joker and widened his mouth.

Joker left the bed again to open a dresser drawer for an unopened block of Kraft's extra sharp cheddar cheese. He opened the closet and reached to take a waxed-paper stack of saltine crackers from the shelf overhead. He came back and laid both in Sweet's lap.

Joker pulled a gold switchblade from his pocket. He flicked it erect and offered the handle to Sweet who slit the wrapper on the cheese right away. He tore open the pack of crackers with his teeth. Joker poured them both more Hennessy then got back on the bed. He shook his head refusing when Sweet extended some of his three a.m. snack. All the while he kept his gaze on the gyrations of Sexual on the floor.

"Hand that broad some reefer. Give her likka, too." Sweet said to Joker.

Audruana inhaled and swallowed. Lying on her back, her sculpted legs hovered spread-eagle. With the V of her crotch exposed showing a little pink patch. She reached between her legs and nastily spanked her secret, lifting her head to watch herself do it. Hungry moans came with every sharp slap, like she was trying to beat down the flames from burning so hot.

"Oh, oh! Whuuut? It's like that? Joker! Go git me some a that crazy broad! She need whippin' by someone qualified. An' I'm the long stroking balla to do it! Three-oh-six, bay-bay! Sweet trey muhfuckin oh to da six! Sekshul…you's jus' lak I lak'm, curved-out!"

Sweet, cheeks crammed with crackers and cheese sprayed crumbs as he spoke. He swallowed a gulp of liquor, parting his flabby thighs made a V of his own on the bed. He shoved cheese in his mouth, chewed and his hand fumbled at his crotch.

"Joker, you's my man! I'm ready to git some, dog. Go git her like we mean it, boss! Put her back through the flo'!"

He looked down at his tugging fist.

"Oh girl, I'm a ride the tas'e out yo' mouth tonight! I'm a git so deep in it, my big boy gon' be deep down yo' th'oat! Make you give me head in reverse an' shit!" Joker guffawed at the humor.

His cock's man sat on the side of the bed and removed his socks without saying anything. Reaching behind his neck, Joker opened the clasp and released the diamond name. He flung the heavy platinum on the bedspread and undressed slowly. Four eyes gazed steadfastly on him.

Of course his tall, thickly chiseled almond-brown body was god-like. His only body hair was the black curly mass nesting his ram. Audruana saw proof certain that he had an incredibly big, hefty joint. The biggest she'd ever seen and definitely the prettiest. It was already standing proud like a monument. The big round head on a heavy straight shaft, picture perfect. Extra long and thick enough to hurt a woman for real, yes please. She wanted some and then more.

The last thing Joker removed was his hat. He was bald. Taunting cocoa eyes under hawking black brows caught her, took her breath away. Sexual was glad she was still lying on the floor, no worry about falling. It was alright if men came finer than Joker. She'd keep this one without a glance at the rest, thank you. Sexual panted while waiting to give it all.

She quickly popped the sides of the tiny thong. Lifting her round derriere to free the straps, Sexual flung it away. Her eyes told Joker to come to the cat. She was hungry for his joystick.

Joker got on his knees his muscles were tensed as he positioned himself to mount her. He bent Audruana's knees so that her thighs were smashing her ample tits and got between them. His palms rested on the floor beside her shoulders. Audruana's hands ran along the bulges cording rock, hard forearms and biceps.

She wiggled, anxious for his giant then he started loading. He was so hard it touched her hotness like cool marble. His rod buried deep into her moistness. Joker was the first to tap corners in a juicy box that every other thought was round.

"Oh…ah…oh, huh…" she squealed, gladly accepting new sensations that felt like the beginning of the world. She felt the pleasure in the deflowering effects of his pushing. Joker was an amazing partner. She'd never received rhythm like this. She opened wider. Her fantasy displayed in the dance was being made real. Joker rode Sexual like she was paying him per stroke.

"Uh-huh! Git it…git it…uh! Uh!" Sweet grunted in the background.

His voice echoed Joker's every filling thrusts.

"Man, I'm ballin'! Got-damn! I'm in it soo deep…! Sek-shual, talk about it, girl! Talk about my sweet Mandingo pipe! Tell Sweet how you ain't never been done like this! Bus' it man!"

Excitedly, Sweet squeezed the small tube he held and rubbed some cream between three fingers. He put that hand between his spread thighs and rubbed the Sta-Hard on his flaccid member. His chest quickened its rise.

"Huh uh, that's it. Use that big ass." He screamed lecherous encouragements, daring the participants into lewder acts. Sweet 306 needed the scenario to get nastier. He wanted to stir the reluctance of his slow rise.

"Ho-o-o, ye-e-ea-ah-h, take it like that! Like that…like

that…My big sugar stick hidin' way up in that candy! Ye-e-e-ah…s-s-s. You ridin like a machine, Joker! Choke it. Stroke it… Sekshul! Sweet 306 got you open to the bone! Ha, ha, ya lak it? Ya, lak it. Stretching yo' mommy all up in yo back…S-s-s…"

Sweet's head fell back and his eyes closed, his right hand rapidly working. Sweat cropped his thick brow. His eyes bulged when he realized something was happening.

Joker and Audruana didn't hear Sweet. They blasted off to someplace neither had been. Then wham, touchdown, they experienced the best sex yet. This was absolute bliss. The fit was spiritually right, the need greedy. Their sex-x-x-ed was like commitment to religion. They were getting it on in skin-slapping joy.

"Oh yes, oh yes!" Audruana chorused in fervor, enjoying Joker's healing shaft.

Except for the ripe slapping sounds of their urgent lust and unintelligible groaning that escaped clenched lips, Sexual didn't voice her practiced erotic dialogue to hurry him along.

Their union was stroke-perfect and nothing could stop them. They were hellcats dedicated to lust. Joker ground her down to his root. Sexual was split opened to her spine. Her next man would just be a stick, his next woman a bore.

"C'mon twist her like a pretzel..." Sweet commanded they got acrobatic.

Joker put Sexual on her feet then bent her over with her palms on the wall. He quickly plugged Sexual rapidly with short strokes.

"Change!" Sweet yelled.

Joker pressed her front flat on the wall, mashing the side of her face. Biting her neck, he was flush against her back with his arms stretched out palms on the wall. He rotated his hardness slowly against her juicy rear. He pulled back, dipped his knees and locked his rock inside her again, pushing forward, forward, not pulling back at all, his bigness completely disappeared.

The way his thigh muscle rippled with each thrust, Sweet knew Joker was breaking new ground. He saw how his perfect ass clenched and flexed. From the waist down she was throbbing and liquid from her shattering release flowed. Her knees buckled but she didn't fall, Joker held her up on his enormous stabber.

Audruana was like a rag-doll. She wanted him to keep banging her long and strong. Let him split her every day, every which way. She wanted to praise him, wear skirts and no panties forever if she could be with him.

In the street at a crowded bus stop she'd plead for

him, unzipped his pants and backed up on his jumbo, greedily swallowing it inside her. He'd get her right into it, held her down by her waist, slammed her hard and fast. She knew he'd do it.

In a long checkout line in a supermarket, she'd drop to her knees and beg to taste him right then. She knew he'd take out that pretty thick snake so her head could bob until he had to have some. She knew he'd push her on her back and bang her on the floor. She knew he'd do it.

On a rush hour subway, she'd grind him against the doors, take out his piece and yank it until he sprayed into her hand. He'd let her do it.

Wherever, whenever she begged for it. She knew that he'd do it right, slaying her each and every time. They'd be vulgar in public and subject to constant arrest. They'd try sex in the police car. They'd attempt screwing while being hauled to the precinct steps in handcuffs.

Except Joker and Audruana or maybe Adam and Eve, no two ever fit papa in mama like this before.

Still joined, Joker stepped her away from the wall and made her bend over the dresser and hold on. She steadied herself on wide legs with both hands gripping the furniture. He began to thrust. Audruana pushed back hotly, meeting every long stroke, covering his strongman almost before he could give it deep.

Sweet had never seen Joker work a woman this way. Bucking like a wild horse, crazy sweat pouring, passionately staying in the saddle. He was all about fucking Sexual. It seemed nothing else could ever feel better.

"Change!" Sweet snarled excited.

Joker swept her up and sat her on the edge of the dresser. He opened the second drawer so she could rest her heels. Audruana's avarice snaked her tongue in and out of her mouth. He heeded his need to squash her pliant big tits and noisily suck her pebble nipples.

Then he widened her knees and stood between them, placed his hands on her hips and turned up her drooling yummy. It dripped nectar so lusciously that Joker bent and latched his mouth to suck honey cocktail.

Joker let her hungrily lick the sticky gleam from around his mouth. Joker set her hips again and took no time ramming his concrete thickly. She made sure to fully surrender by offering him more with an arch in her back, bracing her elbows and heels to keep his invasion pumping right where it was. Their performance was so robust, the back of the dresser banged against the wall.

Sweet was shouting curses. He struggled to all fours.

Like a randy hog in sparkling diamonds, he crawled to the foot of the bed to see better; to better coach. He wedged his pudgy hand between his chunky thighs and got back to the rapid jacking that had his hanging little chitterling mostly hard.

"Change!" he barked hoarsely.

Joker sat Audruana butt back down on the dresser and eased a long finger in her goody. He pushed up to the last knuckle twisting it back and forth. She humped its rotation and made him add another. His thumb made spirals on her button. His swirling fingers intensified what she almost couldn't stand. Her honey ran down his palm soaking his wrist.

Joker pulled his fingers out gently, threads of nectar laced between them. Joker put his slick palm around his shaft and began sliding it up and down its massive length covetously like he was alone. A demon like hand pulled it. He smiled killing the growl climbing his throat.

Joker stood tall with his feet planted like a warrior, caressing his wood with gliding, kneading strokes. Audruana watched his muscles rippling and his knees finally bend. Joker gave in to his own gratification.

Fully aroused, she used one hand to roughly fondle her swollen kitty. She licked her lips. Joker and Audruana watched each other's hands and their pleasures intensified. They were closing on powerful explosions.

Sweet 306 saw their bodies jerking and would have none of it.

"Change!" he commanded grudgingly. It was too late.

"Ah…ah-a-a-ahs…" Her guttural announcement warned that she'd hit Shangri-la.

Joker stopped abruptly before joining her. He was a pro, Joker mentally iced his finish. His agitated stick protested, moving on its own like a slow metronome.

"Change! Change! Sek-shual" Sweet bellowed to no avail.

Joker put his back on the floor and pulled down facing his feet with her knees on either side of his ears. Her big pretty rump was in his face. He positioned her so his soft-pointy tongue feathered over her hot spot like butterfly wings. Joker lapped her na-na like a thirsty dog at a rain puddle, eating her box down to the frame.

She bent to vacuum him down her throat. There was nothing else but this wonderful dick. She worked him eagerly like she was pulling money from it. What a man! Sexual opened deep throat style. Joker hadn't feasted all he wanted. He widened her thighs and kept playing his expert tongue around her juiciness.

Joker flashbacked to his first real nut while thrilling her. He was thirteen and seduced by a hot fifteen-year-old from next door that both his older brothers were banging. Sometimes his brothers had her together. It was her idea to make him a man. She'd suggested it to his brothers and they'd set it up.

That afternoon Joker had come home from school and this baby-doll was naked on his single bed in the bedroom the brothers shared. They were alone because his mother was at work and his brothers knew to stay away. Laughing at his flabbergasted face, she'd told him that she wanted to give him what his brothers were getting. She was so nasty letting him get his first piece, lying on her back thighs high and wide. Then she commanded him out of his clothes. It was on.

He remembered being so hard he was scared his dick would break. Her velvet tunnel was so amazing, entering her made him shout with pleasure. After three devastating strokes he crashed right away, grunting, releasing hard and long. Joker had felt like he'd been hit by a thunderbolt.

She put her palm on his chest and felt how his heart was pounding. She understood and told him it was alright. After a minute of resting, she put her mouth between his thighs and made him brick again.

Before she showed him how to use it, this girl had said that one thing was true; Joker and his brothers were the biggest she'd ever seen. She wasn't going anywhere. She'd put so much sex on him that Joker's second release had started at the back of his skull.

This was what climaxing with Audruana promised to be. Joker knew that when he let go this time, it would freeze knots behind his eyes.

"Change! Change, change I said."

Joker heard the words but had trouble pushing her gobbling head off his snake. He tried to pull her off by her hair. Quickly he rolled Audruana over on her back. She was writhing on the floor, motioning to him, begging him to go inside. Joker got ready to lay pipe.

He couldn't wait anymore. He needed to ball so bad he felt about to split and hooked her willing legs around his strong back. Freaky delicious, he licked his lips as his deep stroking claimed Audruana. Her healthy ass bounced on the floor. She was as wide open like the smile in toothpaste commercial.

They work on denting a rich spot that was too sweet.

They were about to make nature collide and create the lightning of a massive coming together. Their bodies glowed from sweat.

"O! I…I'm…gon' come! Uh, uh."

Sweet's eyelids fluttered and twitched, he gasped, floundering like a fish on land. The hand jerking his dick-let was a blur. "Git it Joker! Hit it hard. Dog that shit! Lemme…oh… come in yo' mouth…Ye-a-a-ah! You got-damn go-rilla…! O-ooh Hur'up, hurry…"

She pulled apart from Joker like they'd never been together. Steaming below, she pushed Joker away, jumped to her feet and rushed to the queen size bed. She was anxious to taste the filling about to leave Sweet's mini éclair.

Audruana hoped that Joker would leap up behind her and finish what he was doing while she ate Sweet's little coming.

But Sweet 306 roughly shoved eager Sexual out of the way of his true desire. His summons wasn't to hunt for the cunt. He wanted his man. Joker quickly fell on the bed on his knees and hungrily found home between Sweet's thighs.

His mouth covered Sweet's little man and began to suck. His greedy throat enjoyed what it swallowed. A few moments later Joker growled low at his own fiercely pumping seed wildly wetting the sheets. While he loved what his man had just done,

Sweet was mad. He fiercely closed his eyes for a beat.

It was all Audruana's fault, nasty bitch: Nastier than all the others.

The women Sweet lured to Suite 306 were there for Joker to pound to a paste. They were foreplay. Joker was more ravenous for Sweet. The girls were usually unconscious long before now, fucked out long before Joker reached climax. The women were just to make sure that Joker's dick would be a monument with Sweet 306 the avid beneficiary.

Usually the woman was out after banging and was too woozy to recall anything. Joker gave Sweet 306 a good time. Sweet paid him well to do it. It wasn't money that made him relish Joker's brutal assault. Sweet had become his favorite lover. Many times Joker sexed Sweet for fun.

Because of this filthy, no shame, draining dame Joker and Sweet had no time to chitty-bang-bang this go round. She had accelerated their trips, made them use themselves up. Audruana gave Joker's prize a spot it couldn't help but thoroughly take like Sweet's. Sweet didn't get his beating.

Before Joker rocked Sweet he gave him a bonus spanking. Sweet 306 fat butt would wiggle anxiously for the sharp slaps that burned his flabby skin. He protested lustily when Joker's big palm popped his cheeks red.

Sweet wallowed in the surprise of not knowing exactly when Joker would invade his talented throat. His lips would be roughly parted from the widening force of Joker's probe. Then he knew.

Joker jumped on the bed and Audruana watched in shock Joker's bobbing head. She adjusted to the reality and loud laughter escaped her lungs.

Her chuckles joined Sweet's hollering. She witnessed the explosion and saw Joker's throat hold Sweet's come. Then just like that, Sweet was out, slack-mouth asleep.

She leaned over and slapped Joker on his pretty thigh and told him to wipe his mouth. That's what he did before he rolled over on his back with his hand behind his head and stared.

Audruana weighed his long, limp heaviness in her palm.

"All gone, huh?" she asked softly as she massaged it. He had screwed her into soberness.

"Damn baby! You know how to lay pipe!" A smile of satisfaction curled her lips. "You made me come like a machine gun," she said. "You got me on call, for real, for real. I need another appointment with your candy. I'll wait…"

She wanted definitely to stay friends. Her eyelids batted

rapidly. Finally she'd been turned all the way inside out.

She panted, wanting to do it again right now.

"What's up?" She asked shaking Joker's shoulder. "You really done?" She asked again. "Hmm, I like how y'all play. Know how to lay a lady like me. Maybe next time we can go deeper. For real, you dig?" Audruana added with a silly chuckle. "Joker, let me watch you stroke your daddy boss-man next time. I'll get off on it. Now I know why they call him fat-ass-Sweet. Ooh, soft muthafucka, frontin' like he a playa, but got more pussy in him than a damn cat." Audruana continued grinning silly like a school girl. "Does Sweet do girls? I do love me some girls. I get down too. I got a girlfriend named Moulaine. We ballin' all the time. She's my baby-boo and is down for the get down. It don't matter, whatever; she's just like me. I see that you and Sweet ain't got a problem providing the head. Next time, I'll bring some X. I'm telling you, it'll be bodacious party."

She shook Joker's shoulder again. Just once, she really wanted to hear him say something.

Joker never opened his mouth. Stroking his big drowsy wood he moved closer to Sweet. His face remained stone watching Audruana's lips moving, trying to convince him about the next time. Joker looked at Sweet 306 who was rousing slowly. His half-open eyelids fluttered and he moved sluggishly on the bed.

Audruana noticed too and started laughing. She leaned over into Sweet's pleasure melted face, grabbed his chin and shook it until his eyes blinked open.

"When do I start dancing for cheddar?" She snickered and asked.

Joker knew Sweet would soon sit up. He'd be very demanding and hungry. Sweet 306 would then get dressed, go out and eat ravenously. Then he'd come right back to the room and immediately get in him. They'd finish off what they didn't get a chance to do.

Sweet 306 watched Joker ogling the talkative female and sighed.

"Time I put tha' naughty cat outdoor!" Sweet 306 squealed under his breath.

fittin' in
Sharron Doyle

Prologue

I was always too busy being smart. My mother wanted me to be somebody important in life. I had big dreams for myself. Unfortunately, I had self-esteem issues long before I even knew what it meant. That would take me back to birth.

We moved to another part of the county and I found that I didn't feel comfortable surrounded by so many black people. I am a black female who was raised around white people for so long, that I started to believe that I was white. I didn't fit in with young black girls and I didn't want to. They were different than I was. I spoke proper diction and they called me a weirdo. The nerve, they were ghetto and uneducated. After the first year I decided that I wanted to be just like them. The effort of trying to fit in played a major role in my demise. My name is Jasmine and this is my story.

First Time

I was supposed to go straight home from school, but like always, I went when I wanted. I was with two friends. We went to school in Chester and had stopped at another friend, Linda's house. She came to the door all smiles as if she had not had company in ages. I remember walking right to the kitchen where another girl was sitting rolling a joint in Top paper.

"What's up y'all? Sit down," she ordered.

"What's up home girl?" We chorused.

We sat and talked about who the cutest boys in school were and agreed on the same ones. Most had girlfriends, but these girls didn't care. I wasn't having sex or even smooching with boys yet. All my friends were coming to school with hickies on their necks. Everybody knew they were doing *it*.

Linda lit the joint and took a long toke. Then she took another and another before passing it. I was the third one to hit the joint. Having never smoked before, I was hoping that I didn't choke. I watched the other girls do it and tried to do it like they did. Needless to say I choked, and kept on coughing. It was embarrassing and I wanted to leave immediately.

"Do you want some water?" Cherie asked.

"Yes, please," I answered between coughs.

We walked to the kitchen with Linda following us like an emergency room nurse. After drinking the cold water, I started giggling as if I was at a comedy show. Linda and Cherie stared at each other. Their actions made me laugh even harder. I was convinced that my new Black friends were indeed morons. In the middle of the laughter, I kept thinking that these girls were from broken homes. There was no joy in their childhood.

Wow! I thought to myself. I couldn't imagine life without laughter. After totally embarrassing myself in front of my new girlfriends, I attempted to pull myself together. I wiped tears from my eyes, straightened out my blouse and picked up my pocketbook that had fallen on the floor.

"Are you alright, girl?" Linda asked sounding irritated.

"Of course, girl," I said sounding like I had planned everything.

"Oh okay then," she said before walking me to the door.

It was a nice way of telling me that I had laughed myself out the door. I told them that I would call them later after I finished my schoolwork. Oops! Confusion registered on their faces. I guess that schoolwork was as foreign as laughter. Poor girls, I thought to myself as I walked down the porch steps.

I proceeded to fall down the steps. I didn't think that a person could fall down steps. Linda and Cherie stared at me in disbelief. Then they both started laughing. I got up with all the self-assurance I could muster.

I got home in one piece and all I wanted to do was eat and go to sleep. I had cereal, French fries with extra ketchup and chocolate milk. My taste buds were out of control. I couldn't decide what I wanted to eat next. I ate everything I saw.

I slept until my mother came home from work, helped her with dinner and went back to sleep. I had no desire to smoke again.

Hangin' Out

Fridays, my mom worked all night and everybody hung at my house. I had started drinking beer. I liked the way it made me feel and I was able to do all the things I couldn't do sober.

Talking to boys was high on the list. I never felt pretty. When I was close to drunk, I'd say whatever was on my mind. The more I drank, the more shit I'd talk.

I was feeling comfortable around my newfound friends. I got courageous and decided that I would take the next step; losing my virginity. All the girls were doing it so really I had no choice. They'd finally accept me in their crew. Now, the least I could do was go all the way. The girls were pressuring me because I still had not done *it*.

"What are you waiting for?" They asked.

"Yeah, what am I waiting for?"

I was dying to get a hickie. It was the only thing left for me to do, then I'd totally fit in. I knew that once I did *it* I'd be one of them. I couldn't wait. The first time I tried I didn't like *it*.

Experimentin'

I never understood what people got out of doing blow. I tried it and couldn't breathe. It made my nose drip and left a horrible taste in my throat. I kept spitting, but the taste was still there. That was the best part of the high, the girls told me. As far as I was concerned it really sucked.

When Victor put coke in a cigarette, I liked that high better than sniffing. I stuck with that while the rest of them sniffed. After a while, my stomach was so upset that I had to go to the bathroom and puked. Nothing but liquid came up because I had not eaten since lunch time at school. Mommy was working a double-shift so the crew and I had been at it for hours. It was now four in the morning and time for the party to come to an end. Mom would be getting off in three hours. I still had to clean up and hope that I could look normal when she returned.

I looked like a skeleton. I vigorously scrubbed my face with soap and water as if I could wash the look off my face. I forced a bagel down my throat and drank some tea, then started cleaning up. There were empty beer bottles and coke bags all over the place. My friends were pigs. I could not believe that they had just thrown shit all over the place as if they were in a park. They had no respect for my crib. I bet they wouldn't throw trash all over their moms' house.

Checking the clock I could see that it was damn near seven. Mom would be getting off work any minute. I called to ask her if she wanted me to make breakfast. I really wanted to know if she'd left work early. I got in bed and turned on the TV. I'd do this on a Saturday morning if I was up. I didn't want her to be suspicious. I looked like I had been up all night and concocted the lie of the century just in case she questioned why I looked so tired.

Mom came in at her normal time and called out to me. I tried to sound as groggy as I could, indicating that I had just woken up. As usual, mom came in and looked in my room. She kissed my forehead before going into her room and stripping out of her clothes. I could tell that she was exhausted.

I got out of my bed and moved next to her. I massaged her shoulders and back. She sighed in relaxation, and I gave her a full body massage. I put baby oil on my mom's dry feet and rubbed them until they were soft. Before mom went to sleep she commented that I smelled like beer.

"We'll talk about it when I wake up," she said sleepily.

Damn! I'd forgotten that she knew everything.

18

I spent my eighteenth birthday with Linda and Cherie over at Juanita's house. Juanita's house was where everybody hang-out and shoot-up, or smoke rock. Her grandmother had passed away and left the house to her. The house was beautiful but after some time, it looked like a junkie's habitat. Anything illicit, from drugs to tricks and dealers, was found there.

I had been staying there on and off because my mom had kicked me out when I was sixteen years old. She could not take me getting high anymore, because I was killing her. I tried to understand what she was going through, but I just couldn't.

Much had changed in the past few years. It happened so fast that I really didn't know what hit me. I was caught up in drugs and lost my identity. There were times I'd stare in the mirror and wonder where the years went. I looked old for my years. I felt used and warped. Drug abuse and prostitution had beaten up my once young, innocent body. I had been through it all.

I started turning tricks early in life to support my coke habit. I had a heroin addiction that kept me on my knees and back. I didn't blame my mother for throwing me out. I'd have done the same thing if I were in her position. It wasn't until later that I understood what she meant when she said: I was killing her. Mom couldn't bear to see me destroy myself. Part of her was dying with me.

The evening of my sixteenth birthday I was hanging with my so-called friends. One of them passed me a pipe. He took the foil out of his jeans pocket and put two pieces of rocks in it.

"Here cutie," he said with a friendly smile. "Blast off."

He waved the lighter like it was a magic wand. I wanted to try it and took the pipe.

"Thanks," I said leaning back and taking a hit. The rock was good, melting as soon as the flame made contact. I exhaled and was caught up admiring the smoke disappearing. I wanted to fade away. I no longer wanted to be here. I spent another birthday away from my mom. She was the only person I ever really loved.

"How was it, cutie?"

I heard him asking through my thick dark cloud. Did he really care? I sneered with disgust. Deep inside controversy lurked. I managed to flash a pretentious smile. I had practiced the routine to shield me from the torment I felt.

"It was good," I nodded.

Out of nowhere, he leaned and kissed me on my neck. Maybe it would've felt good, but I was high and didn't want to be touched. My stiff reaction warned him against trying that again.

"Damn cutie, you're too tense. Let's go get a room and I'll massage your back." He winked. I was captured by his eyes and sexy smile. "What do you say?" he asked reaching for his coat.

"Yeah, that would be nice." I heard myself saying and rose. I'd rather spend my eighteenth birthday in a clean room than here with my junkie friends. Nobody had spoken to me since I got here. I wanted to leave.

We got in his car and drove to a Red Roof Inn off the expressway, mostly occupied by travelers. There were no junkies. The desk clerk gave us a look that was everything but inviting, with a tight smile to match.

"May I help you?" She managed to ask.

"Yes, we would like a room. Something away from the expressway if that's available." My date responded.

"Of course sir, do you have three pieces of identification. One with a picture and two credit cards?" she asked derisively.

"Is there a registration form that I should be filling out while you check my cards?" He asked sarcastically.

I smiled when he slid the plastic across the desk to her. We stopped at the soda machine and got a couple of cans. He held my hand intimately. I strolled to the room. It felt good.

The room smelled fresh he turned up the air conditioner. I got in the shower. After that he gave me the best massage. He kissed my back and worked his hands down to my butt cheeks.

"Would you like me to continue?" he asked.

Wow! I was stunned. So much respect it had me tingling all over.

"Yes, please," I sighed enjoying it. My body was so relaxed that I had to fight to stay awake. I'd been up for three days and my body was suffering from sleep deprivation. "Oh yes, ugh…" I moaned when he kissed my back again.

"Get some rest, cutie. I'll have something here for you to eat by the time you wake up," he said. I felt safe and fell into a deep, pleasurable sleep.

I felt him pulling the covers over me and kissing my forehead. I felt the tear rolling down my cheek.

"Happy Birthday, Jasmine." I whispered to myself.

Free

"Hello! Good morning, housekeeping." The yell came from outside the door followed by banging on the door.

"Just a minute!" I yelled back.

I got up from the bed, walked to the door and checked the peephole.

"Ma'am, do you want your room cleaned?"

"What time is check out?" I asked her.

"Your room has been paid for another day. Do you want me to clean it?" She asked again.

Paid for another day? I wondered to myself. I remembered him saying overnight when we checked in. I opened the door.

"No, thank you. Is it possible that I have some fresh linen?" I asked. The housekeeper turned up her nose at me and passed me clean sheets with towels before turning on her heels.

I stood in the middle of the room looking around trying to remember the last thing I did before I fell asleep. I walked over to the bed and saw a note.

My date from last night had to leave. He paid for another night. According to the note, there was money and heroin under the mattress. I looked and they were there wrapped in tissue. I put two hundred in my pocketbook. The dope was on the bed. I remembered the massage and going to sleep. The food was on the nightstand. I couldn't remember if he did me while I was sleeping. I hoped he used a condom.

I ate, cleaned the works and tied my belt around my arm. Having selected a good vein, I pricked my skin with the needle. Hoping that this was good dope, I shot up. On my back, I let the heroin course through. My body shook and my eyes settled in the back of my head. I went into convulsions right before I blacked out. Those were my last moments of freedom.

Mom

I stood watching mother scrambling eggs in a bowl with pepper and grated cheese. While she waited for the butter to melt I placed my head on her shoulder. We sat at a table in the dining room and looked through the mail. Mom always waited for the last minute to look at the mail unless it was a bill. Mom drank her coffee. I kissed my mother on her forehead.

"I'm sorry." I said. She did not respond. I walked to my room crying like I'd never cried before. I was wiping my eyes when I heard a car. I got off the bed and looked out the window. Two men in suits were getting out. The doorbell rang, and my mother's voice called out, "Who is it?"

"Police, ma'am, we're looking for Joanne Reyner."

I sat in the recliner listening to the detectives telling mom that my body had been found in a motel.

"We need you to identify the body," the detective said.

Mother's shriek of agony brought neighbors running. One caught her before she passed out. I wish I could have told my mother not to mourn my death but rejoice it. No longer

would I have to worry about fittin' in.

birth of a gangster bitch

Princess Madison

I was thirteen when it happened, an ex-friend of mine chatting me up as I walked into the school building.

"What did you say, bitch?" I asked as the school bell sounded.

She ran off without responding and I chased after her. The bitch must have dipped into a hallway locker or sump'n. I went all over the building searching for her. We were from the same projects and always attended the same school. That evening I went to her building but she wasn't around. The next day I searched the halls at the school looking for her. I made a bee-line as soon as I caught sight of her and was all up in her grill before she could say boo.

"What's up with you?" I said accosting her.

"What's up? What's up?" she recanted not backing down. "Why you invading my space, bitch?"

"I heard you going round dipping your nose in people's biz, bitch."

"I ain't said nothing nobody don't know bout you. I known you a long time and I for sure know you got a whorish mother."

"Bitch you talking 'bout my mother like that?" I asked removing my earrings.

I stopped close and center. I wanted to get off the first punch. It was gonna be a good one, I thought looking in her eyes.

"Whatcha gon' do bout it," she threatened taking one too many steps till our noses rubbed like Eskimos kissing.

I swung immediately decking the bitch. She fell dazed in the school corridor. I was on top of her unleashing lefts and rights in rapid succession. Before I knew it, the fake ass school security bum-rushed me and held me good until the cops arrived. They let her go. The tin badges put me in the cruiser. They drove around telling me all this bullshit about being good and all that.

I really wasn't trying to hear what they had to say but had no choice. So I listened to their lecturing.

"Nobody is gonna get away with calling my mother a whore." I said.

They decided not to arrest me. The girl did not press any charges so for my own good, they escorted me home. When we reached my mother's apartment they knocked and we waited outside. Her red eyes were wide and she looked scared as hell when she answered the door.

"Ms. Jennings we brought your daughter home because she was involved in another scuffle at school. This is the third time that we've been called to the school. You've got to keep a better eye on her."

The officer spoke to my mother in the hallway. When they were gone I walked in and smelled why she was nervous. The smell of marijuana lingered crazy all over the apartment. I was ready for her when she jumped in my shit.

"Amila you gotta do better girl. You cannot be getting into fights everyday it's just not right."

"Why are you yelling at me? I didn't start it."

"What did that girl say that cause you to go nuts breaking her nose?"

"She tried to diss that's all," I replied shrugging.

"Everyday it's the same thing you ain't nothing but trouble, girl."

I stared at my mother and felt pity. I didn't want to tell her what caused the problem. She needed someone around to protect her. Furthermore, no one was gonna disrespect my mother and get away with it. If I had to fight everyday to keep the haters away, so be it. I was thinking along those terms when I saw another man walking out of my mother's room. I turned away and shook my head in disgust. Without saying anything else I went to my room and slammed the door.

It was a different man everyday. Sometimes it was two or three different men. Different complexion, some fat, some skinny but always there was somebody. They all wanted to spend their money for her time. She was my mother.

At first, I honestly thought that it was because my mother was beautiful and sexy. She had long toned legs that led up to nice, firm, brown ass. Her long hair bounced to the rhythm of her sashaying hips as she moved. I knew there were men who just straight up dug being with a pretty woman. As far as I was concerned, it didn't matter. I didn't want to hear anyone talking mess and if I did hear that shit, I'd be on them like stink on shit.

Couple weeks later in school, the same fat-head chick tried to set it on me as I left school. So I followed her and her friends around the corner and off came the jewels. I jumped on her swinging wildly. I don't know where all this anger be coming from but I handled mines when I got down. She kept trying to pull my long braids. I beat the shit outta that bitch. By time five-oh came and dragged me off, her nose was bleeding real bad and her lips were busted. This time they took both of us down to the local precinct. All the time they kept repeating the same question:

"Why are you two dealing with each other like boys?"

"Are you girls, young ladies or thugettes?"

Call me whatever, I don't care, I thought coldly staring at her lumps. All I knew was the bitch had it coming. Now just let me out of this car so I can murder this bitch. I shot her the look of death as I was thinking.

They took us to the precinct and we sat around waiting. We were in a cold stare-down, me and this bitch. She switched up quick and started bawling loudly when her mother came. Her mother was telling five-oh that she wanted to file charges against me for assaulting her daughter.

"This is the second time this little bi..." she started.

The police waved his hand stopping her. Then they gave her the papers and locked me in a cell.

When my mother came they told her I couldn't file charges against the bitch. I was furious. Imagine, she started it and I couldn't do anything. When I got home nobody could say shit to me. No one did. That evening my mother broke out with her date like nothing was wrong.

"Stay in and do your homework. I'll see you later." She smiled as if nothing was wrong. The most important thing on her mind was being with a man.

"Mom, where are you going?"

"Amila don't ask me those types of questions. This is grown folks business, alright? Do your homework and then get some sleep."

She fixed her make-up and was out. I ran after her yelling.

"Mommy, how could you just leave without not even kissing me?" I asked hugging her. I loved my mother.

"Here, baby," she said stooping and landing a wet one

on my cheek. "All right get back inside and make sure the door is locked, okay sweetheart? Mommy will be back soon enough," she said and was gone. The fragrance of *Wild Orchids* trailed after her. That's how it was. Mother worked her charms on these men with money and got her fair share at the end of the evenings.

Most weekends, mother would be gone Friday and Saturday. She'd return dog-tired on Sunday morning. I'd be left to do what I wanted to do, alone at home. It should've been a happy time. Imagine being home alone and doing whatever you wanted to do, every weekend. The situation was every teen's fantasy but those weekends were the worst times of my life. There was radio, television and reading. The fact is, I was lonely and needed something else to keep me busy. I took up smoking and although I hated to do it, I'd seen mother seemingly enjoying it. Soon I learned to like the fact that I could inhale without coughing my eyes watery. Next I started drinking. Pretty soon I couldn't wait for mother to leave on her dates. I resorted to helping her get out the door of the apartment with the quickness.

"Why are you rushing me off, Amil?" she asked without

the slightest hint of suspicion.

"I just learned that Black people have this bad habit of being late for everything and I'm trying to clean up the act of everyone around me." I smiled.

"Clean up your act first. You just gotta make sure you get to school on time, girl." Mother chuckled and waltzed out the door.

As soon as the door was shut, I raced to the bar and poured myself some Disarrnao. It was sweet, palatable and didn't burn my stomach. Lighting the cigarette, I held it the way mother did. I swirled the thick drink, just like she did with my pinky finger sticking out. Then I threw my head back and laughed just like she would.

After two drinks I'd get tired of the mimicking. Over a month, it became three or four glasses before I'd get sleepy. Everything including sleep started going down easier. I no longer sat around waiting for mother to get home but was fast asleep couple hours after she was out the door.

Some mornings I'd awake feeling nauseous. In class I felt at any minute I could sneeze and my whole head would go up in an explosion. This was my introduction to drinking. Looking forward to my next drinking session allowed me to hide the truth behind the wry smile I wore publicly. I called it dealing with reality. Others may call it alcohol abuse.

I thought that beating her ass would be the end of that and I resigned to the feeling that the bitch had the ass-whupping coming. I arrived home about six o clock about a week later to find my mother's name tagged all over the building. 'Sheryl a ho' was scrawled on the side entrance, on the bullet-in board in the lobby and inside both cars of the creaky-ass elevator. My first thought was to go upstairs and see that bitch, who was now fast becoming my most hated enemy.

We were a very happy family. My parents gave me the best and everything seemed to be going well. Then came the day I saw my father's head blown wide open in front of me. I died a sudden death inside when I was forced to watch as my mother was raped repeatedly by who I thought were looters. I found out later through the police that my misfortune was an actual hit. I hated my mother after the discovery. They'd lied and covered it up well. It took the death of my father to unleash a sincere desire to get even with all those who perpetuated fraud.

Mother was still being a whore even after I graduated. I wanted to leave home. She didn't want me to. I must have wanted to stay. I spent the summer after graduation thinking about leaving.

It happened late Friday night. Mother was on her way out. She was getting ready.

"Amila do not stay up all night. Keep the door shut."

"Okay, I know." I answered watching her carefully putting on mascara.

"Mommy, why do you have to go out?"

She stared at me and smiled. Mother was pretty and had a smile that could melt any heart. She had mine. I returned her kiss.

"No more questions," she ordered and wiggled into her tight red dress. A wave and she was gone. The slammed door echoed like the teasing of the neighborhood kids. Your mother is a whore. I heard the ringing in my head and adjusted the volume of the television trying hard to drown their shouts.

I still could hear them playfully giggling from my room. Six in the morning and mother and her companion had returned from being out all night. The sound of sucking lips followed and then heavy breathing. It was then I'd shut out the heavy sounds, hard breathing and animal grunts. Followed by mother's blood curdling screams. The sexual romp would continue through the morning.

Saturday morning cartoon was my escape and I often took it with cold cereal. Later mother and I would go buy the best in a shopping spree. She was sporting a spanking red M6 and I loved when the neighbors stared at us. I hated how mother made a living but I enjoyed the fruits of her labor. I wallowed in the conflict and had huge emotional outbursts with anyone around. This Saturday it was mother's turn.

"Now you know you didn't have to scream at the store clerk."

"She shouldn't speak about things she's not sure of." I insisted and flung my backfield with my stride.

"She made a mistake, she didn't have your size and she apologized," mother said catching up.

"Yeah, but did you see the face she made when she was apologizing. The bitch acted like we wuz after her man or sump'n. She was acting like we some high class hos!"

Mother gave me the evilest stare. Then I felt the sting of her slap. Tears stung my eyes but I bit my lips so hard, I tasted the blood. I faced mother with cold eyes.

"Are you happy now?"

"You deserved worse than a damn slap…"

"Oh yeah, and what do you deserve mother? Aren't you more than a high class ho'?"

This time mother shook her Manolo's off and charged at me. I met her with rights and lefts. We truly had a drag-out fight right there. Mall security came to her aid. I wanted to kill the woman. Then we cried together nursing our bruises. It was a weird day. That night mother couldn't duck out at her usual nine pm time. She sat on the sofa with me drinking hot chocolate and I tended to the shiner I'd given her. I didn't need the alcohol or nicotine tonight, mother was home.

"Where did you get all the anger from, Amil?" she asked looking at the black and blue mark under her eye.

"I don't know mommy. I guess from you," I said applying ice to my shiner and nursing my busted lips.

We sat around watching television. Mother sipped her favorite drinks and smoked cigarette after cigarette, then her cell phone started blowing up.

"I'm not doing anything tonight," she told the caller. She threw the cell phone on the nightstand but it didn't make it. I rushed to pick it up.

"Leave it alone. Throw that damn thing away."

The words had hardly escaped her lips when the phone started ringing again. I gave the phone to her, but she refused to take it.

"Turn it off," she ordered.

I did and we went back to watching television. Mother enjoyed *Sex in the City*. It happened at the end of the episode in the midst of us laughing, the doorbell rang. I went to answer the door. One of the neighbors hurried by me and grabbed mother's hand pulling her towards the window.

"Look, Jen, two men putting a licking on your car."

The woman pointed out the window and mother peeked out as if she was in a nightmare. She pushed the window open.

"Hey, what the fuck y'all doing?"

She ran to her bedroom and came back stomping mad. It wasn't until mother went to the window and started firing that I noticed she had a gun. She kept firing at the street below while the neighbor ran.

"Mother don't you think you should call the police?" I asked nervous but feeling excitement in me building.

"Fuck the police! They ain't gonna do shit for me..."

She kept on busting shots until her gun was empty. There

was a knock on the door when mother ran to get another clip. She answered the door and two men walked in. I felt better as I recognized one of them. I was glad they weren't the police. Then everything went crazy.

"Who da fuck told you you could turn your phone off?"

It was mother's friend who always picked her up. He smacked the gun from her hand. I was gonna pick it up but he pushed me away.

"Go to your room, Amil and don't come out no matter what." Mother ordered me. "I can handle this."

I watched her twisted smile, like a drunk. Reluctantly I walked to the room, closed the door and listened.

The argument was loud.

"I own you bitch. You're my property and I want you to work, you work. No questions. You my ho and a ho ain't got no life but the one I give you…"

I heard him yelling. There was silence followed by a loud thud. I waited then heard the door slam. I opened the door and walked out to see mother lying on the floor.

"Ma," I screamed.

She didn't move. As I got closer I saw the scarf around her neck. It had been pulled so tight that it left marks around her neck. I loosened it. Mother rolled over her eyes bugged out and her body cold.

"Someone help me please..." I ran off to get the phone.

As a cop I discovered the connection and who ordered the hit. I had to make a decision to betray my badge or continue to help those who had killed my parents.

Watch out for *Gangsta Bitch* the most compelling story of its time.

two mothers

Vanessa Martir

Butch

"Her mother's a butch, yo," said the fat girl wearing thick glasses.

"Get outta here! I didn't know that! Her mom's a lesbo? Ain't that sump'n?"

"Butch doesn't mean lesbian!" I shouted. Perplexed, I turned and look at them.

"Yes it does, stupid. What'd you think it meant?" The fat chick retorted sneering.

I stared at the cold cafeteria food. It was just seconds earlier that the pepperoni pizza looked really appetizing.

Suddenly, it didn't look so good. I was in the fifth grade sitting in the lunchroom when my friends made me realize I was growing up in a gay relationship. I recalled the many times I'd heard my mom and Aunt Millie arguing. Mom would call Aunt Millie out of her name.

"I'm not a fucking maricona, puñeta! I'm a butch!" My Aunt Millie would yell.

After the name-calling incident at school, I viewed those words and moments entirely different when I heard my two moms arguing.

I started seeing them for who they were. Like when I witnessed the first erotic moment involving my two mothers. Mom, my birth mother, was leaning on the washing machine smoking a cigarette. She casually parted her lips and inhaled while she watched Aunt Millie walking towards her. I saw her through a cloud of smoke simpering seductively as Aunt Millie leaned the weight of her body on my Mom's, opened her mouth and swallowed her tongue.

I never gave a second thought to my home situation. In my mind it had become normal despite reality. You'd think that I'd consider it odd since on TV all you saw were heterosexual couples. I don't even recall the moment when Millie became an aunt. All I remember was growing up creating Father's Day cards for Millie and Mother's Day cards for my mom.

What I distinctly recall is that it was turning to Aunt Millie for comfort and understanding. When I wanted something so bad, it hurt, I'd go to her. That's how I got my rainbow bike.

Yes Guy

Poverty is hardest on children. They don't understand when their parents can't buy them the things they desire and have yet to grasp the concept of a budget. Aunt Millie tried her best to shield me from the disappointments of impoverishment. I'd turn to her whenever I wanted something. She'd always say yes.

I became obsessed with bikes when I was eleven. Resentfully I'd watch the neighborhood children riding up and down the block. I daydreamed of having one. I didn't fantasize about an expensive Barbie bike like the one owned by Melissa, my nemesis of the block. She had a gorgeous, shiny pink bike with white tassels hanging from the handlebars.

It didn't have to be one like that, just a bike. If I asked my mom, she'd scream on me. She'd remind me of how selfish I was and that we could spend the little money we had on more important things. Then she'd recount one of her horror stories, growing up in abject poverty in Honduras. There it was considered a blessed day if one went to bed with a full belly. Of course everyone in my mother's immediate surroundings in Honduras was dirt poor. It was easier to deal with, I thought. The commercial world we lived in made it worse for me.

We're first generation American children. We've got televisions advertising all the toys and games that cost money, which my mom didn't have. This became quite a challenge for my mom. As a parent who endured growing up in an underdeveloped country, she wanted to give us what she never had and more.

Realistically, however, she could not do so. My mom had a difficult time coping with this. When I asked her for anything, she became angry and defensive then would lash out. She felt guilty about her inability to grant me my wishes. Her way of dealing with it was to make me feel bad. I caught on to her scheme at a young age. Then I learned that I was Millie's weakness. She'd do anything to see a smile on my face and hear a shriek of glee echo from my lungs. It was to Aunt Millie I'd turn to at my moments of need.

I'd go to her whether it was a pack of Now-N-Later candy, or a pair of sneakers. Aunt Millie would go out of her way to please me. Knowing this, I would always hesitate to ask for expensive items. Despite her weakness, I didn't take advantage. When I could no longer bear Melissa's smug smirk, I broke down and told Aunt Millie I wanted a bike.

Rainbow Bike

It was a hot summer day. The kind where the heat rises from the asphalt and your Mr. Softee cone melts before you can take the first lick. Melissa was riding up and down the block with a snide grin on her face. I watched covetously. It didn't matter that her bike was pretty. I wasn't like the rest of the little girls on the block who touched the bike tenderly with eyes gleaming with jealousy, and pleaded with their parents to buy them the same one. I was green-eyed at the fact that she had a bike. That's all I wanted. Finally, I decided to approach Aunt Millie.

She was sitting on the front stoop eating a piragua, a ghetto treat. Aunt Millie was wearing her usual pair of old jeans. Her key ring hanging from one of the belt loops seemed to contain a trillion keys to my eyes. I heard them jingling when she exited the building. I stood anxiously at the door waiting like a pup awaiting its owner.

Aunt Millie smiled when she saw me. My lips tightly pursed as I conjured the courage to make my request. She often surprised me with how well she knew me. Together we sat sharing her tamarindo piragua. She watched me as I gazed at Melissa riding up and down the block. Aunt Millie scolded when I stuck my tongue out at her.

"¿Que te pasa? Ese huevo quiere sal."

"Millie, I wanna bike." I whined.

"What kind of bike do you want, one like Melissa has?"

My face beamed when the question popped. Millie laughed when I wrinkled my forehead and shook my head in disgust.

"No! I want a different bike. I want one just for me."

She said nothing and sipped her shaved ice, savoring the sweetness. I pouted and walked away with my head down. She's not gonna get it for me, I mulled disappointedly. For some strange reason, I'd rush home everyday after school, expecting to find a bike waiting for me. I daydreamed about one day coming home, finding a bike with a huge red bow around the handlebars and a license plate with my name engraved.

Weeks of disappointment and crying myself silently to sleep rolled by. I gave up on the idea. I even stopped staring at

Melissa's bike. I simply didn't want to give her the satisfaction of knowing that I was sweating her bike.

Shortly after the school year ended, I noticed Aunt Millie working in the backyard. The last time I'd seen her working so diligently with her tool kit, she'd nailed a bike rim to a slab of wood and improvised a basketball rim. This make-shift net allowed me to play with the Spalding basketball she had splurged on. I excitedly climbed out the window and sat next to her. My eyes bulged and my young heart raced relentlessly.

Aunt Millie was putting the finishing touches on a bike. The body was a dazzling purple color. One wheel was yellow, the other red, the seat was black and the grips, which were peeling away, were a pretty aqua color. Aunt Millie didn't even look up at me.

"This is for you negra," she said with a chuckle. I could feel the sweat on her upper lips when I kissed her. I hugged her so tight she almost lost her footing.

"Ho, ho, ho," she laughed heartily like Santa. Aunt Millie stared at my beaming face with satisfaction. Several minutes later she helped me carry the bike through the window and out onto the street. She watched as I clumsily coasted down the block with joy.

I found out later that she had gone around to her friends and neighborhood junkyards collecting bike pieces, and slowly but surely gathered enough to put my bike together. Several days after she gave it to me. I awoke to find rainbow tassels on the ends of the handlebars. That was all she could afford to buy, plastic strings in various colors which she put together to create tassels for the bike.

The minute I rolled down the street on my bike, Melissa started laughing and insulting me. The boys began to call me Rainbow Bike and created a song to the tune of *Rainbow Bright*, the Saturday morning cartoon show. I brushed off their teasing and rode my bike with such pride that you'd think I was riding a royal chariot. Soon, all the kids on the block fell in love with my bike.

I'd race and beat anyone who challenged me, except of course the boys with their ten speeds. Friends wanted a ride and when I was preoccupied with playing handball, tag, double-dutch, tag football or any other game, I'd lend it. It was the greatest moment.

Slap

Melissa was angry that no one was envying her little Barbie bike. She hated me before I had my bike. Her revulsion intensified. All the attention and admiration of the neighborhood kids fell on my Rainbow bike. I was riding up and down the block when she appeared out of nowhere and maliciously rammed into my bike.

"What the hell is wrong with you?" I screamed.

She laughed and sped off. Melissa knew that if I caught her I'd beat her to a pulp. I'd done it to her more than once. Normally, that's exactly what I'd have done. On this particular day, retribution was farthest from my mind.

I stood in shock and horror. My mom had put me in Bible study classes several months before. Unfortunately, the God I'd been taught about was not a merciful, loving God, but a vengeful, unforgiving God. I feared Him more than I feared the Devil himself. I even had nightmares about the world being destroyed by the wrath of God and me sizzling like a roasted chicken in the infernos of hell.

My fear of God made me obsessively cautious about the way I behaved and even the things I said. My impressionable mind was convinced that God would sear me if I offended Him in the slightest manner. That day when I uttered those words to

Melissa, I became petrified that God would send me hurtling to the bowels of Hades. I was unsure if what I'd said was a sin and wondered if God would understand since I'd said it out of shock not malice. I cried until my body shook and prayed until my little hands were blue from being tightly clenched together. I decided to consult my mother. I was sure she would advise me properly as to what God would do and think.

That night, my cousins came to visit from Long Island. This was always a fun time for us kids. The women would get together and cook while the men and Aunt Millie played dominoes. The children were left to tend to themselves and do what we were all notorious for; causing mischief.

We lived in a tiny railroad style apartment so the succulent fragrance of sofrito in beans and meats and the crisp smell of white rice boiling, wafted easily throughout the apartment. The aromas were accented by the sound of the dominoes being shuffled and slammed on the table.

"Capicú!" shouted a player.

My cousins were playing with the Atari and tousling around but I was distracted. I kept staring at my mother in her yellow stained apron, wondering what she would say when I told her. I was hoping she'd comfort me and ease my fears. I felt I had sinned and needed my mom to tell me it was okay. I had not done so out of spite and was not a bad girl. God wasn't going to banish me to el infierno.

Finally, the nerve to talk to her came. I slowly walked to the kitchen and sat beside her.

"¿Que quieres?" she asked in frustration. Busy preparing the meal, mom hated to be disturbed.

"Ma something happened today I want to talk to you about ..."

"¡Avánza! ¿No ves que estoy cocinando?"

"W-w-w-well," I began stuttering. "I was riding down the block and Melissa came and bumped me on purpose. Look." I said pulling up my pants leg and showing her the black and blue of my swollen shin. "I yelled at her, W-w-w-w-what the h-h-h-hell is wrong with you?'"

In a split second my mother's face changed to every color in the spectrum.

"What the what? What the what?"

She curled her lips tightly, exposing her clenched teeth and roared. Before I knew it, she had backhanded me twice across the mouth with hands coated with cow's blood and sofrito.

The silence that followed was deafening. All the happy

chatter that emanated from the living room suddenly ceased. The jangling sound of the dominoes halted. All I heard was a litany from mother.

"Tu eres una fresca! Cómo te atreves!" Mother's loud admonitions shook the apartment.

I learned that I could never confide in mother. She was not the person to turn to when I needed comforting and reassurance. I also found out that day that she thought I was a wicked little girl.

foolish pride
Joy Leftow

Poverty is not noble at all and doesn't choose color. Felix wasn't a drug dealer when I met him. He only decided to be one when he learned how tough it was to refinish furniture all day. He roughened his hands just so he could pay the rent on a small, overpriced room in Harlem.

I was sitting on the front stoop, high from the amphetamine I had swallowed earlier. I was playing with my three-year-old niece, Brianna, tickling her and leaning her backwards until she squealed.

"How does this feel? Do you like this?" I asked. She was giggling crazy when I swung her around.

Just then Felix walked by with my friend Chatter, he

never shut up. Chatter had been hitting on me for about a month but I wasn't attracted to him. Both were wearing bell-bottom jeans. Felix had a two-inch decorative trim going down the seam of his pants on both sides. It was a pretty embroidered Aztec design and was mostly gold in color, mixed with orange.

Felix had dark olive complexion with a wide nose. His eyes were so dark they looked black with Indian features. He had long, black, curly hair. I've always been a sucker for long hair.

I sat down with Brianna's legs around my waist and leaned her backwards. I was wearing a tank top and low rise hip hugger jeans. When I leaned forward with Brianna on my lap, both guys got a good view. I was cute with dark brown long hair. I wore bangs in the front and red highlights. I had a petite figure and rosy colored skin with blue eyes that frequently changed to green. My tits were small and I had big hips with a small waistline.

"Hey," Chatter said. "This is Felix, my friend from Santo Domingo."

I extended my hand and Felix kissed it. I sighed as his action took my breath away.

"You're the most beautiful woman I've ever seen. Why don't you and I disappear somewhere alone for a minute," he said looking into my eyes.

Where was this dude coming from? I'd just met him. I was thinking. He moved really fast.

"Let's take a walk through Ft. Tryon." Chatter suggested.

"Sounds cool. Let me take my niece inside and I'll be ready," I said.

We entered the park and headed for the stonewall. It overlooked the Hudson River and the GW Bridge. Chatter waved to some guys toking a doobie. Chatter was well known. He was the LSD connect up here.

I was walking in the middle between the two guys. Chatter saw Felix put his arm around my waist and he caught feelings and came between us.

"How bout some ice cream?" Felix asked. Chatter immediately followed.

"Do you want ice cream, Janis?"

"Oh yes, I want a cone," I said taking out my purse. Felix put the cone in my hand. He winked at me and patted my hip where my purse was.

"I got it, babe," he said.

Felix put his arm around my waist and slid it towards my

butt as he steered me towards a bench under a flowering apple blossom tree. He immediately sat next to me. Chatter was still getting his ice cream.

"You're cute and all, but you move kind of fast. Do you mind?" I said moving his hand off me.

"I can't help it, you're just that hot." Felix smiled.

"Are you staying at Chatter's?"

"No, I got a room in Harlem."

"That's fast work, how'd you do that?"

"I read El Diario, that's all."

"Since you work so fast, any leads on a job yet?"

"Is this twenty-one questions?" He grinned.

"I'm just wondering how a foreigner gets around," I said.

"Hey man, I gotta go home, my mom's cooking." Chatter interrupted. He looked at me pointedly. "So you gonna be home later, or what?"

I stood up not quite knowing what I should do. I knew Chatter was feeling me. He introduced me to Felix who I was now feeling.

"So what ya gonna do?" Chatter asked.

"What's the story here? Maybe I'll just head on home

myself."

"Where ya going so fast ma, we just met?" Felix asked grabbing my hand and pulling me back down on the bench. "Let him go. I wanna talk to you alone." He leaned forward and whispered. His breath was soft and warm on my neck. I felt goose bumps all over my body along with Chatter's intense stare.

"So what you gonna do?" He asked.

"Stop tripping. You know you don't invite anyone to eat your mom's food. We'll catch you on the rebound." I said.

An awkward moment of silence followed as Chatter surmised the situation.

"I'm out," he said, turned and walked away. Felix patted my hip.

"You really wanted to get rid of him didn't ya'?" I asked and we both laughed.

"It's not my fault he's got his priorities crossed. I mean what's more important, a woman with the most beautiful blue eyes on the planet or a meal? Hey weren't we in the middle of a conversation?"

"Yeah, I wanted to know; how did ya get a room so quickly?"

"The woman who owns the apartment was in Santo

Domingo two weeks ago and we kind of set it up then. As far as the job goes, she introduced me to a furniture maker. I've got a job refinishing furniture. I'm starting on Monday."

"That's cool, so you're set then."

"All except for a woman. Now I met one."

"You've got it all figured, huh?" I shook my head smirking.

"I got it figured out even better now," he said looking me up and down.

After that Felix was at my house every night without fail. I shared the apartment mom had when she died two years ago with Hanna, my older sister, her husband and child. I slept in the living room on a single bed. Hanna took over paying the bills after mom died.

I was nineteen years old and had a lot of problems. I had already been pregnant twice and lost the babies. I had no education to speak of. I lived in the same apartment where I had lived since I was born.

Not to be outdone, Hanna and her husband, Freddy had a shit load of problems too. He was just like dad, a compulsive gambler.

Hanna was a strange case; smarter than me with no

education either. She was almost finished getting her high school diploma. I still had history, math and science credits to complete.

I met Freddy first but had no interest so I introduced him to Hanna. She fell for him on the rebound. After her last and only relationship, she spent a year in the apartment depressed. I did all I could to move her back into circulation.

I kept moving but way too slow. I had a part time job downtown as a receptionist and I took evening classes in theater. My dad paid for that. It seemed now that since he retired and was receiving social security, he was doing a little better. I was eligible for welfare and got fifty dollars a month.

One evening I was sitting on my bed holding hands with Felix. He was in the midst of expressing undying love for me. We had only known each other a couple weeks.

"I can't stop thinking about you. It's like I'm going crazy when I'm not with you. Why don't you marry me and spend the rest of your life with me?"

"You're crazy, Felix. I mean like we're together two weeks and you wanna get married?"

Hanna came traipsing by. Carrying a non-spill cup of warm milk in her hands, she paused and stared at us. My sister's curiosity made me very uncomfortable.

"I'm having trouble getting her to sleep. She keeps playing and singing. I'm so tired."

Hanna was trying to drum up some small talk. I wanted her to keep moving.

"Hey Hanna, how ya' doing?" Felix greeted.

She nodded, moved on and he continued his romantic overtures.

"How much better do I have to get to know you? I've seen you every single night this week and last week too."

"Well," I giggled. "You still don't know me in the biblical sense."

"Freddy should be home soon." Hanna said as she walked by once more.

No sooner were the words out of her mouth than we heard the key to the front door.

"Hey baby, I got lobster for you. I hope that does the trick if you get my drift." Hanna winked and Freddy flirtingly smiled and sidled up to her. He waved and immediately turned to follow her into the bedroom. His hand rested on her butt, goading her along.

"Back to our conversation. I'm trying to figure out that

biblical part."

"What's stopping you?" I challenged.

"I can't just bring a blue-eyed honey like you into Harlem."

"A blue eyed Jewish girl like me? What's up with that? I grew up in this neighborhood. All my life I've hung out with blacks and Latinos."

"I've got a surprise," Felix said smiling. "I'll tell you later."

I started thinking about his proposal and how crazy it was.

"You're fucking with me to get your green card. That's what's up, ain't it?"

"No, ma I'm crazy about you. I had a green card before. I lived here when I was a kid, so the number could be reactivated. I'm for real. I want to marry you and get old together, spend the rest of my life with you."

I jumped up and he did too.

"You are so full of shit. Do you think I'm stupid? And you think I got nothing better to do than think about getting old. You're pissing me off."

I resisted when Felix grabbed me and started kissing

me.

"Don't worry, you'll learn to trust me," he said.

"You must be crazy. You think I really wanna think about being a hag. That turns you on or sump'n'?"

He laughed and placed my hand on his dick. It was rock hard.

"Just being next to you does it for me, even if you're across the street. I get hard when I see you. I can't wait till I hit that."

"Seems like you've been waiting just fine to me," I said laughing.

"Yes, but now the owner of the apartment is leaving for a week. It's the perfect time. I'll pick you up on Friday after work."

"Why don't I just meet you at your place?"

"No way, I don't trust that. You alone in Spanish Harlem? I'll pick you up."

"Whatever," I said nonchalantly.

He rubbed his hands together, made circle with his finger and poked another finger through it.

"I tell you, it's gonna be like the fourth of July."

"Can I count on that?" I smiled flirtingly.

"Yeah," he grinned, "and then we can get married."

In spite of my tough act, I was sensitive.

"Don't make fun of me and don't play me!"

"I'm for real. I'm dead serious. I want to spend the rest of my life with you."

"If you keep it up, you won't see me again. No one just up and marries someone like that." I said snapping my fingers.

"They do if they're as sure as I am. I want to spend the rest of my life with you. Most girls would be happy if their boyfriend proposed."

"Right, but they'd be happier if they believed it was for the right reasons."

"If you marry me we'll move to Santo Domingo and buy land. We'll build a nice house and…"

"Why would I want to do that?" I jumped in.

"Baby, it's a tropical paradise. We can lie around all day, go swimming, eat coconuts and mangos. We'll live like the original natives did."

"You're gonna build a house too?"

"Your body will turn firm and brown. You'll be even more beautiful than you are now. You'll be like a goddess."

"The first fucking man who begs me to marry him and

you've got to be a joker." I shook my head in disbelief.

"You'll see."

When Friday rolled around, I was hot to trot. As we walked into the apartment, I kept up a constant chitchat.

"Why did we have to wait to come here? Aren't you allowed company in your room?"

"They're really old fashioned and an older couple. They'd get mad if I bought a girl here. They don't believe in sex before marriage. And I think they'd expect me to date a Dominican girl.

"Oh yeah…?" I asked staring at him incredulously. "You mean brought a girl here. I sarcastically corrected him.

"Yes, sure... Would you like some juice or something to drink?"

"Nah, I was hoping for fireworks and a band."

"Come here," Felix said and held out his arms.

We sat on the bed and started kissing. I pulled away. Something seemed a little weird with his kiss.

"Why don't you open your mouth more?" I asked.

"My mouth is open as far as it goes," he said frustrated.

"I feel like I'm fighting to get my tongue in there. Look, like this," I said spreading my lips.

"Your lips are wider than mine," he said.

"Wait a minute." He walked away to the bathroom.

I stripped down to my lacy black underwear. Felix came back and lunged at me, diving on the bed.

"Hey, take a breath. Take off your clothes so I can feel you. Do you like oral sex?"

Felix stiffened. "I don't do that. I had a bad experience one time."

"You had a bad experience one time and that turned you off forever?"

He nodded.

"So what happened?"

"It's kind of embarrassing. I did it one time and uh..."

"Well what is it already?" I asked impatiently.

"She had sores and my mouth got blistered and the doctor said it's quite common and not to do that..."

"Really, well the doctor never told me that. I mean shit if you did catch a little something, penicillin is all that it takes. That's a real drag."

"How come?"

"Because I really dig it," I said unable to hide my disappointment.

"I don't mind having it done." He jumped in smiling.

"Right, leave it to a guy. Man, I used to go with this dude and he'd..."

"Shut up about these other guys, I'm going to make you come."

Felix mounted me, moved a few strokes then groaned. This turned sour really fast. I attempted to push him off, but he locked his legs around mine.

"Please, don't push me away. I couldn't help it," he begged.

I was turned on and curiosity got the best of me. I touched him.

"I can't do it again right now. I've been working all day and I need to rest."

"OK maybe not this instant, in a while then." I said and did nothing to hide my disappointment.

"Yeah, in a... What's this on the sheet, blood...?"

"That's what happens from my IUD. It makes me pretty much staining all the time. I can't figure it. The doctor said I shouldn't worry about it."

"You're bleeding all the time and the doctor said not to worry about it?" he asked jumping out of the bed.

"Hey, it's not contagious."

"That's some crazy shit ma. You better get checked out again. I don't know what kind of doctor would say that's ok. Oh shit!"

"You're over-reacting," I said.

"The family I live with, they're gonna see the blood on the sheets when they come to change them."

"So?"

"They'll know I bought someone here and even worse, they'll suspect it was a virgin."

I was feeling disgusted and disappointed. My big expectations for fireworks had taken a downward turn.

"Big deal," I said with no sympathy.

"It's a big deal for me. I live here. Hey don't you have any money to go to a real doctor?"

"I do go to a real doctor. He prescribed this method of birth control for me."

"It's not normal to bleed all the time. Maybe you've got some infection or something," he said acting concerned.

"Listen, I do get checked regularly. Matter of fact they already took out the coil IUD and now they put in the S shaped IUD. They said the last one caused an infection and they scraped me out. They said maybe this one would be better."

"You're telling me this has been causing you trouble since day one and you're still using it. I don't get it. Why?"

"Mostly because it works and I just get pregnant too damn easy. That's why the doctors recommended it. I was pregnant twice before. I was only fourteen the first time."

"What happened?"

"My body aborted, I was too young."

"Let me give you some money so you can go to another doctor. Get some birth control pills. That way you won't have to be going through this bleeding."

"You my gynecologist, or sump'n?"

"It doesn't take a genius to see that you bleeding all the time isn't normal. I'm telling you, let me pay for a doctor and you can get the pill."

"I don't want the pill."

"Why don't you want the pill?"

"There's a history of breast cancer in my family. My mother died from it."

"What's the pill got to do with breast cancer?"

"Some doctors say it's not good to use the pill when there's a history of breast cancer in your family. There's concern about the hormones in the pill causing the disease."

"Hey, my stepfather's a doctor and he said there's no real connection."

"Okay, I'll ask about the pill when I see the doctor."

"Let me know the cost."

"Oh yeah, you wanna pay?"

"Yeah, you're my old lady now."

"Don't worry about it, I've got Medicaid. Thanks for your offer."

Felix's eyes were closed. He had fallen asleep. His hands seemed raw and bruised from the day's labor. I stared at him before going to sleep.

Next morning I tried to give sex another try. I'd been around but I wasn't a ho. I was sexually aggressive when I had a man. I jumped on top of Felix and started riding him. Two minutes later, I heard him groan.

"Damn! You came again." I screamed still bouncing up and down trying to hold his erection.

"It'll get better after you get that thing out of there," he said rapidly losing hardness. I was disappointed.

"I gotta pee," I said.

"Hurry up, I know this great Dominican cafe on the

corner. You're gonna love it."

Certainly no fireworks I thought while hurrying. Taught me that when a man brags about his shit, it's because he ain't shit. More important to me was that Felix needed me. We both needed love. Figuring I had nothing to lose I stuck with him. The sex was pretty bad, but most people can learn techniques of lovemaking.

After a while, it seemed like a good move to leave Hanna and her family alone. I tried to find my own place. It wasn't easy, especially when funds were low.

I kept in touch with my friend Carmen. We'd known each other since Public School. Carmen was Boricua, pretty, six-feet tall with big hazel-brown eyes. She had a little too much weight.

Carmen was pregnant and lived in a horrible basement apartment on One-sixty-third and Amsterdam Ave. I decided to stay with her so I'd have more freedom. She hated Felix.

"Girlfriend, I don't know what you see in him." Carmen would always say. Money was too tight to hassle.

The first day Felix walked me home we were attacked by a group of young men. Felix managed to fend them off then we were started running.

I was high on acid and pot and was having difficulty turning the key to the upper lock of the basement door.

"The bitch got keys," one of the guys yelled.

We got inside, ran through the basement to Carmen's door in no time. Felix was hot on my heels.

The weather had begun to turn chilly. Felix and I had been together for six months. I would see him often enough. We'd talk and he'd tell me everything. One day he went off to see a compadre from Dominican Republic. He left to score some LSD. Felix was doing everything to score.

It shouldn't have been a surprise when Carmen came running at me.

"Did you read the newspaper today?"

"No I answered."

"Felix got busted. Read it," she said shoving the paper in my face. My heart sank and all hopes faded as I looked at the news report.

Felix Pratts-Figureroa and Juan Ortiz-Martinez, natives of Santo Domingo, were intercepted yesterday when police were called about a party in an apartment on Park Avenue South. The parents of the minor, who cannot be named, were notified and the minors were all taken into custody to wait pick up by their parents.

"I told you he was a loser. Forget him!"

I didn't want to but he needed help so I went down to court and met him. He was booked and released on his own recognizance.

Visits from the INS man with cold blue eyes became frequent. It chilled me to look at him. He said if I didn't marry Felix, it was likely he'd be deported. Carmen was totally against the plan.

"Don't marry him please!" She screamed.

After Carmen gave birth, her family let her back home. Soon after, her mother gave up the apartment to Carmen. Couple months later, Carmen gave it to Felix and me. People in the hood got to know us and no one bothered us. The rent was something ridiculously low. Later HUD declared the apartment inhabitable and we moved to an SRO.

We lived at the Rio Hotel on Fort Washington Ave for about three weeks. Felix and I walked the streets everyday looking around Washington Heights. I'd visit my sister and we'd walk all over the Heights.

One spring day, Hanna and I stood outside a street level apartment between St. Nicholas and Audubon. I saw Chatter. He was parked and chatting up a sexy Latina. He turned and looked at me from behind his dark shades. Chatter was dripping with bling hanging from his arm and neck.

"Hey it's my Jewish chick," he greeted distastefully. My sister walked away and Chatter approached. "Still sexy ass," he smiled showing more ice.

"Hey Chatter, I see you're doing well," I said and felt the girl's eyes probing.

"Real good," Chatter said and gave me hug. "What're you up to these days?"

"I'm trying to make it..."

"If you come with me, I'll take care of you for the rest of your life. I got all kinds of paper..."

"Let's go Chatter," the sexy Latina cooed.

"I got biz to take care of," Chatter said getting into a new BMW. He waved and left us choking in the fumes from his exhaust.

"Drug dealers," Hanna said shaking her head. "They live so good."

We stood watching the dust settle and I was thinking about what could've been. The door to apartment opened and we raced inside to see the super.

I knocked to get the attention of the guy painting. He turned out to be the landlord. I got the apartment and Hanna landed a city job with HUD. She became the landlord's personal secretary.

Here I was, after being with Felix for a year, with my own apartment. The walls in the living room were made of brick. There was a huge closet off the living room.

I was still getting my little bit of welfare and working part time jobs. Sex had gotten a little better but Felix still hadn't gone downtown yet. I was hot and could usually get off without much effort. I was young and wanted to enjoy sex the right way by playing and experimenting. He was my husband and Felix was the person I should be able to get nasty with, but he didn't want to.

Money was a problem and I was disgusted because no matter how hard he worked, Felix never had enough dough. My sister and her husband, Freddy, tried to help us. They rented carts and we sold ice cream in Central Park. When winter rolled around Freddy switched to pretzels and chestnuts plus he had a sideline business selling knock-off perfumes.

One day as they were all seated at the table, I walked in proudly and made an announcement.

"I started that temporary job with the census department today and interviewed an old lady on Fifth Avenue in a beautiful apartment. She invited me in for something to drink. And guess what? She grew up here and wanted to know all about the Heights.

"How long will that job last?" Freddy asked.

"Two months at the longest."

"What about you, how'd you do?" I asked Felix.

"I made one hundred and twenty five bucks today," Freddy said.

"That's good." I said hugging Freddy.

"And I really want some good weed," Felix said.

"C'mon man, don't you have any of that stuff around?" I asked.

Felix started to roll a joint.

"Hey, what's up with that?" I said, "Freddy says he got one-twenty-five, what you got?" I asked staring him down.

"Bitch, what you mean what I got. What the fuck you got?" He wasn't very tall, but he was threatening standing over me.

I smacked my lips in annoyance. Freddy came and stood between us.

"Chill out," he said.

Felix stood at the table and continued to roll.

Fuck, this shit-head smoked from the moment he got up till he went to bed. I was fuming as I sat watching.

"I got twenty-five," Felix said.

"Goddamn! You gotta have more than that?" I said.

"Leave me the fuck alone," he said as he threw four nickel-bags on the table.

Freddy put his arm around me to slow me down.

"Where's the rest of the money?" I asked shaking off Freddy and walking to the living room. I saw some new items on our small living room table. A shiny new brass Buddha, a dormer and a meditation bell along with another new book about Buddhism.

"Man, you're a piece of fucking work. We're living off my welfare which pays the rent and the rest. You have to be high twenty-four-seven. That's where all the money goes." I was screaming at Felix. Before I realized what hit me, the sting of his slap burned my face.

Freddy was there in a second.

"What the fuck you think you're doing Felix? Back off and chill out!" He screamed and grabbed Felix.

"He ain't got no money and he don't even try."

Thank God Freddy was there because my mouth kept going.

"You're sitting on a gold mine with this Acapulco gold you scored. No one else I know got this shit, man. I don't know why you're messing it up. I'll be your first customer. Go and get half a Z." Freddy said interrupting the fracas.

"He could if he ever kept any money lying around long enough to," I said and Felix glared at me.

"What're you saying?" He asked.

"Shit, a fucking week ago you spent one hundred and fifty dollars on an ounce of good pot. It was gone in two days."

"And you did nothing to help me lose this pot?"

"I hardly got to taste it, because this selfish bastard kept it all to himself. He just smoked and smoked continuously until it was gone, you just can't stop. I mean I like to take a hit a day but not all fucking day long like you..."

"You smoke heavy too", Felix said.

"Yes I do. After I realized that it was almost gone. I shared two joints with you, big deal."

"Hey man, I got enough money to buy some. Go and score some right now. I got an idea Felix, tell her she can hold on to the weed and control it. That's the only way you're going to get her to go along with this." Freddy said winking at me. I smiled.

"You're such a bad girl!"

"Yeah well, its best I control it because he'd smoke it all up and we'll lose money. Freddy you got a good point. Everyone I know says the same thing about how good this shit is."

"Besides," Freddy said to Felix ignoring me. "Janis is real friendly and talks to everybody. If you let her hold it, she'll help you because she knows a lot of the dudes hanging out on the corner right now. She can talk to them and tell them to buy it from you."

"So now you think I wanna be a drug dealer, huh? End up in jail too right. You guys are unbelievable." I said shaking my head.

"From what I've read, the Feds are only interested in the hard stuff, you know cocaine and heroine."

"Yeah, so you've read. Show me the proof," I said.

"I will," Freddy said.

"Sure, tell me anything." I laughed.

"You ain't gonna get rich on your census job," Felix said.

"You're not likely gonna get rich on dealing weed either. You're gonna smoke up all the profits."

"Oh really…?"

"Yeah," I answered sarcastically.

"It could be a lot of fun."

"And a lot of fun getting set-up and busted too."

"I've got forty dollars to spend right now. How much you got Janis?" Freddy asked.

Felix looked at me.

"C'mon man, gimme the cash. I'll let you hold it as soon as we get back, I promise. I mean really we do know a lot of heads, and I really think this is a good idea. Janis, baby, I'll let you hold it. C'mon baby - give me the money." Felix pleaded.

"What the hell. Either way you're gonna do it. So I may as well help you. Otherwise this'll be a losing proposition here with all the profits literally up in smoke and you in jail."

I wasn't just smarter. Everyone says they're smarter. I mean I'm smarter in the street way. I'd learned to survive. I'd been through a lot of shit way before I'd met Felix. I'd escaped scathed or beaten but always lived to tell the tale.

You never know how far a road will lead in the beginning. Then you put some effort into the journey and you see how wide that road can grow. That's just how it was for us. This drug peddling thing took on a life of its own and expanded beyond our wildest dreams.

beautiful bird

Genieva Borne

It was the wee hours of the morning and the bottle of Viagra sat on the night stand next to the lamp.

"I thought this stuff was guaranteed to work."

Rodney picked it up and flung it against the wall. The little blue pills spilled from the bottle to the floor.

"Maybe you're just tired. We've been up all night trying and you've been working very hard lately trying to get your security business started. Just relax and who knows, it'll kick-in." Trina spoke softly trying to console her fiancé.

Rodney got out of the bed. He walked to the bathroom and slammed the door. He stood looking in the mirror, nothing but his birthday suit on. Damn! It's bad enough I'm not hung like those gorillas down at the prison, but now you don't even want to get up for my girl. He thought as the disappointment caused by his lack of manhood stared dejectedly back at him.

Lack of confidence wasn't a suit Rodney wore well. He held his little man in the palm of his hand and shook it while looking in the mirror. Frustrated, he smacked it.

Trina was a beautiful and shapely woman. Her perfectly shaped almond eyes were soul-piercing. Her long wavy black hair that she got from her mother's Cuban ancestry, and the large, round bottom that was standard on her father's side of the family were a perfect mixture of her Cuban- African American heritage. Sweat poured from her warm, caramel complexion. Gorgeous, she sat on the bed yearning for her man in between her thighs. Rodney was twelve years her senior and used to make love to her everyday. Then he had the hunting accident.

Trina went right back to consoling Rodney when he came out of the bathroom.

"Rod, listen I know you're upset but we can keep trying. The doctor said that because of your damaged nerves, the Viagra wouldn't necessarily work all the time. If we keep trying maybe something will happen. Baby I need you to make love to me."

"If you love me, you're supposed to love me for other

reasons, not just how I fuck you."

"No, I didn't mean it like that."

It was five a.m. and the alarm clock buzzed. Time for her to go to work, she thought when she saw Rodney wasn't in a good mood. Trina was tired from being up all night. Lately, it seemed all they did was argue over his sexual performance. She didn't want to do it this morning.

Trina went to the closet and began to dress for work. Rodney became increasingly frustrated as he watched.

"Maybe it's those fucking ugly blue uniforms you wear everyday. When are you going to quit that freaking job? I hate the fact that you work there, around all those filthy animals. That turns me off. You like being around all those diseased rodents looking and gaping at your ass don't you?"

"Rodney, why are you tripping? I met you at the prison, right? You were a corrections officer working with the same filthy rodents."

"Things change. You're my fiancé. My wife shouldn't be working behind prison doors. That's why I'm busting my ass to get this security company off the ground because with my job, my properties, and my cell phone business, I make enough money for you to quit that job now."

"That's just it. They're your companies and your money. What about my own money, my own job. I so happen to like my job."

"I don't understand why any woman would want to work around criminals and murderers? You must like being in the presence of those animals."

"Rodney, we're not even married yet and you're already trying to control my life."

"What do you mean not yet? Are you trying to say that you're reconsidering marrying me?"

Trina paused then let out a sigh.

"No, I just don't want to quit my job before we get married. If something happens that causes us to break up, I would be out of my job. Besides, I like earning my own money."

"Trina, we'll never break up. If you leave me, I'm sure I'll do sump'n very stupid."

"What do you mean by stupid? Are you threatening me?"

"No, all I'm saying is don't ever think about leaving me because I couldn't imagine living without you."

He was acting strange and Trina was very uncomfortable. Four years ago, his ex-wife told her about his controlling ways.

At the time she chalked it up to the venom of a jealous ex. Now Trina was feeling that it had some merit.

She was glad he had changed to nightshift so that he could run his businesses during the day. She couldn't stomach the thought of working the same shift as him and then dealing with him at home.

Around six a.m. a kitchen detail slid a tray with a couple of rock hard pancakes and some watery syrup under the door.

"Breakfast," he yelled.

The deep sound of his voice echoed off the walls awaking Dorel. Four white walls stared back at him when he opened his eyes. Things were the same for the last three years. One look at the breakfast made him loose his appetite. He kicked the tray to the corner of his cell without a bite. Like every other morning before, his mind replayed the bad event that brought him here.

Why did Rome have to start shooting at me right in the middle of the hood over that bullshit? The thought haunted his mind. The little girl would've never gotten shot. He was transported back to the fateful day. He was walking to his car when a black BMW Jeep pulled up. Bullets suddenly started flying in his direction. Dorel ducked behind his limited edition Jaguar and tried to retaliate, but couldn't get a clear shot. Bullets flew at him like missiles that had locked in.

Dorel was able to let off three times, then saw a dumpster near a building that was being reconstructed and decided to run for it. She was walking down the street when shots following Dorel hit the little girl, sending her body flying backwards. A cold shiver surged through him when the memory flooded his mind. One more year, he thought looking at the marks on his wall.

Dorel's parole hearing was due next year. He hoped that what happened in his first year of his incarceration wouldn't hinder him from getting paroled. He started at Sing Sing but ended up breaking another inmates arm and fracturing his spine in a fight. He had been on good behavior and out of trouble for the three years of his stay at Coldwell. He found something that he liked very much; a bird.

Every morning he prayed for thirty minutes then did two hundred push ups, two hundred crunches and rounds of shadow boxing. Dorel was in the middle of his one hundred and ninety-eighth crunch when he heard the sexy voice.

"Pipin state your ID."

He paused at the voice, but put in his last two crunches.

"4-2-9-2-8-8...how are you doing today, bird?"

Trina Evan's eyes glanced at the clipboard then looked at Dorel's six-pack. He was about six feet tall and perfectly toned. He rocked a low cut Caesar with razor thin sideburns that ran down strong jaws. Dorel noticed her checking him out and smiled as she quickly lowered her eyes back to the clipboard.

He imagined her out of her uniform. The uniform did nothing to conceal the fact that she was a most beautiful woman.

"Pipin, why do you always call me bird? The name is Officer Evans."

She could see the bulge in the front of his sweatpants. Pretending not to notice, Trina tried hard not to stare.

"Like I said the name is Officer Evans. You know if I really wanted to I could put you in the hole for insubordination." She snapped in a sassy tone

"Sorry, you caught me out there," he said clearing his low raspy voice.

"It's no big deal."

He grinned because he knew she liked what she saw.

Dorel uncovered his erection and it hung in full glory. She glared in shock. He winked his eye at her to let her know, she too was busted.

"Is that what you want, bird? Me up in the hole?" he asked lowering his eyes to her midsection and licking his lips.

"Don't play yourself Pipin. You know what hole I'm talking about. You won't be joking when you're locked up in there."

He smiled. Flirting with Evans was part of the daily routine.

In the courtyard...

Recreation was for one hour everyday. Inmates had the choice of going outside to exercise, catch fresh air, or stay indoors watching television or playing card games. It was basketball season and today was the big tournament. All the inmates were outside to watch the game. Most had a special interest in seeing the game.

Tarva Witherspoon was playing. Everyone had there money on him because he was sure money. He was a legendary high school player at Canarsie High School. He had every college and an impressive amount of NBA scouts seeking him out. One month before graduation, his cousin and him were pulled over and busted carrying four keys of dope. Tarva got hit with the max. Whenever he played, everyone put their money on him.

It was a beautiful sunny day on the courtyard, a perfect day for a game. Dorel just like all the other inmates of this segregated unit wouldn't dream of missing this game, but not for the same reasons as the others. He didn't put any money on the game. Dorel knew that Tarva was going to throw the game in order to make all the money off the odds. Dorel couldn't help but watch the interesting chain of events that would go down around it.

Dorel didn't sit directly in the mix of the crowd because he preferred to observe his environment rather than blending in. Besides, today his bird was on yard duty. He sat off to himself to make sure he had a clear view of the courtyard and her. Dorel liked when she was in the yard, he could admire her. He saw Evans standing behind the fence.

Dorel was staring at her hoping she'd look his way. She spotted Dorel looking at her and turned her head trying not to stare at him. He caught an erection watching her.

The game was about to start and the crowd was getting amped. Dorel heard another prisoner asking.

"You want to bet on this game my nigga?"

"I ain't ya nigga, Hector. You got one second to unblock my view or I'll put you on your ass."

"I was trying to let you get in on some money."

"Hector, you taking shit too personal."

"What you say nigga…?"

"Didn't I tell you I'm not your nigga?"

Dorel gave the man a serious body blow to the stomach. He dropped to the ground gasping, and Dorel stomped him right where he was hurting. The man puked breakfast and some blood along with it. Dorel was so smooth with his knuckle game no one saw.

Evans saw what had gone down. She was about to signal for help, but Dorel looked at her and blew her a kiss. He placed one finger over his mouth before she could. She turned as if she didn't witness anything happen at all. He walked away inconspicuously and blended into the crowd.

"Hector, you alright man, who did this to you?"

Hector was unable to answer. His cronies looked around and saw that Dorel was the only one who had moved across the yard. They knew something went down between Hector and Dorel. They weren't about to start beefing with Dorel over Hector's dumb ass. They picked him up and helped him to a bench. Another guard that was patrolling asked Hector what happened.

"Those nasty ass pancakes ya'll serve this morning for breakfast got my stomach fucked up."

The game was over: Tarva threw it. The only ones who was not surprised at the ending was Diesel and his crew. One by one they walked back into the building cursing about the game. Dorel passed Evans and gestured as if blowing her a kiss. She blushed. He knew he had her where he wanted her.

The next day when his bird arrived at Dorel's cell he wasn't doing his usual exercises. He was still in his bed. He appeared to have fallen asleep reading a letter, there were a few sheets of paper covering his chest.

"Pipin, up on your feet," CO Evans ordered.

Dorel looked up and saw the corrections officer.

"Good morning, bird," he smiled flirting.

"You're not exercising this morning. I guess she kept you up late, huh?" Evans joked.

"Who kept me…what?"

"The love letter from your girl," Evans said.

"I don't have a girl."

"Oh, you have girlfriends?"

"The only girlfriends I have are Ms. Lefty and Ms. Righty."

Dorel gestured as if beating off and Evans chuckled.

"I see you in here writing everyday, and don't tell me you're writing to mom."

"Well, you assume that I'm writing letters to women telling them how much I miss them and how I want to come home to them and only them. I'm surprised bird, I keep telling you I'm not like all these other guys in here."

"So what do you write?"

"Poetry…"

"Yeah right," Evans said shaking her head and was about to walk away.

"Hold up, I have something to show you."

Dorel Pipin handed her the pages. Evans began to read it. It was a letter from a congressman thanking Dorel for writing him letters about his concerns on issues. A menace to society he was, but he cared about the future of other young black men who could change if given the right chance.

"Okay, you got me. I'm impressed. But you don't spend all your time writing to politicians concerning our youth and our community. I know you throw a kite out every now and then to some chick."

"Let me show you what else I write."

"Trust me, Dorel it's not even necessary."

"Oh, but I think it is."

He pulled a thick black spiral binder from under his bed and handed it to her. It was covered from end to end with words. She slowly turned the pages of poetry. One page in particular caught her eyes.

"Do you mind if I read this?" She asked.

"I've always wanted you to."

She turned her eyes back to the poem and read it.

My little Bird

In this dungeon I live

A life not worth spit

no air, without light, or love,

I survive cause of my little bird,

Mornings she's at my window

Like a ray of light

Her delicate wings carrying hope,

Despair when she's gone

so goes my sun, my air.

Every morning helplessly I wait

unable to breathe till she smiles.

Her heartbeat I feel knowing

hers beats and so does mine.

Till the end of my time always

She'll be my beautiful bird.

"Dorel, is that why you call me bird? Is this poem about me?"

CO Evans blushed when she asked the question. Tears appeared in the corner of her eyes.

"You know you are my beautiful little bird." He said placing a hand on her soft cheek.

"How did someone like you end up in here?"

"I didn't have a beautiful woman like you to keep me humble. I thought I could rule the world alone." He said touching her hand.

She felt his words hit her heart like an arrow. She pulled her hand back, afraid of being vulnerable.

"I have to go finish my rounds," she said.

Later that day Evans came to Dorel's cell. She opened the door.

"Pipin come with me," she said in a firm tone.

"Why? What's going on?"

"I'm taking you to the doctor."

"Why? I didn't put in a slip. I'm not even sick."

"He's pulling you for a routine check up."

He followed her out of his cell and through the prison. She appeared tense and overly cautious, glancing around like a thief afraid of getting caught. Dorel became anxious but didn't say a word. She led him to a part of the prison that he'd never been. They continued down a vacant hallway to a gray door. She motioned for him to stop and pulled out a set of keys. Evans quickly opened the door and pushed Dorel inside.

"Where are we?" he nervously asked.

"Shush! This is the psychiatrist office. He's out due to a car accident. For now no one comes here. We can be alone here."

"How did you pull this off?"

"Because I'm engaged to the captain, I can get away with anything without being questioned. I've covered all my tracks." She nodded.

"Bird, are you sure you want to do this?"

Evans unbuttoned her blue uniform shirt revealing see

through fiery red laced bra. Most of her perfectly round c-cups were exposed, her hardened brown nipples strained against the transparent fabric.

"Dorel, I see the way you look at me, and I know how you feel about me."

He held her face and looked in her eyes. Dorel couldn't believe his bird was in his hands. Unzipping her uniform pants, he unbuckled her belt. Her pants fell. His eyes bugged when he saw her matching red laced thongs.

He touched her love spot. Evans was wet. He nibbled at her nipples and felt her quivering all over. She was out of her bra when Dorel sucked her breast in his mouth. Dorel ran his tongue all over Evans breast, licking her neck. Evans aggressively pulled Dorel's wood out of hiding.

"Hmm…" she sighed and smiled when she saw the size. Dorel had something to offer, she thought as she slowly stroke it. On her knees, Evans brought his erection closer to her lips. She kissed it and struggled to adjust to the size. Halfway in was an accomplishment, she worked her lips. Dorel closed his eyes and opened them again and again.

She sat on the desk the psychologist used for analyzing patients, opened her legs wide and gave Dorel a clear view of her waxed, love box. He smiled at the sight, knelt and tasted her. She squirmed barely keeping her body from sliding off the desk. Dorel picked her up and laid her on the sofa. He rubbed his pole on her thighs and clit.

"Oh…yes give it to me…" she begged.

She grabbed him and pulled him into her world. Dorel thrust inside of Evans womb. He wanted to release the pressure he was desperately trying to hold back.

"Bird," he moaned.

"My name is Trina. I want you to call me Trina while you make love to me."

"Trinn-na-na…" Dorel whispered in her ear.

She bit her lip holding back the screams. Evans shoved her tongue down his throat to keep from screaming. Dorel hadn't had the beautiful feeling of being inside of a woman in three years. He held on to his erection with great anxiety as he thrust into Evans' tight, warm wetness. He didn't want to release early and was determined to make this last as long as she could handle it.

"Oh yes, oh yes, ah yeah…" Evans moaned approaching a climatic zone.

Dorel assault on her g-spot levitated Evans. A flush came

over her leaving her faint but stimulated.

"Damn!" she sighed.

Soon after, his love juices erupted like a volcano. Dorel immediately tried to reinsert. Evans wasn't having it.

"Come on Dorel, we've to get back before anyone notices we're missing."

Dorel pulled up his pants, Evans was about to open the door. Dorel was dazed.

"Dorel, what's up? Why are you just standing there?"

"Before we leave I need you to answer this question. Why are you taking this risk? I know that you fucking with the captain."

"Dorel, can I trust you to keep your mouth shut?"

"You trusted me enough to bring me here."

"Yeah, well this is really personal." Evans paused and swallowed. "Captain Sweany and I have been having problems for a while. I love him but lately I don't feel the way I used to about him. I find myself anticipating coming to work just so that I can get to your cell and see you. Some of the things you say, and that poem you wrote for me, made me feel something I haven't felt in a long time, and that's beautiful."

"Are you sure he's not cheating on you?"

"He was shot in his left testicle a few years ago in a hunting accident. It had to be removed and the surgery left nerve damage. He has a problem holding an erection for too long."

"Are you sure he's the right man for you? Can you go the rest of your life with a man who can't please you?"

Trina put her head on Dorel's muscular, sweaty chest and contemplated what he had asked her. She had asked herself that question many times, but didn't want to think about leaving Sweany.

"Dorel, you make me feel special, and I wanted to make you feel as good as you made me feel. That's why I'm taking this risk. You are worth it to me."

Dorel left wondering if Evans was being sincere or was it the sex talking after he had just finished turning her insides on like a faucet.

The weeks passed and Trina Evans found new ways of getting Dorel out of his cell for pleasure, twice weekly. On days that Sweany was out of town, she pulled doubles just to creep with Dorel. She made it her primary focus to figure the times and places they could hook up. They had sex in empty closets and unoccupied offices. Whereever she could get the bone.

This day made the third day in a row that Trina had

gotten Dorel to take him to one of her secret places where they'd spend time alone. She was on top riding and bucking, Dorel hit her switches, taking her to the highest peek of ecstasy. CO Evans closed her eyes and rested her head on his muscular chest. She was breathing softly when they heard the voices of guards just outside the room. She was just about to explode. He paused for a moment.

"Oh, baby, I'm about to come. Please no..."

"Don't you hear?" Dorel asked trying to get from under Evans.

"They're not coming in here, they're just passing by." Evans said not wanting to stop. She pushed Dorel back.

He pushed her off of him and she landed on the concrete floor. The loud voices outside the room were now far away.

"Dorel what the fuck did you do that for?"

He walked over to her to help her to her feet and console her.

"I'm sorry Bird, but I had to get you up off of me. You were attacking my joint. Didn't you hear those guys out there talking? We're in a fucking prison. I'm the inmate and you're a guard. Don't you know we playing with fire? You can't be slipping up like that, bird."

He had to keep a clear and focused head. No pussy was going to take his mind away from his real goal.

A few months later, things had cooled, but Dorel had Trina on his mind all night. He hoped that she'd be able to get him alone. He wanted to hit it in the worst way. He smelled her shower gel when she entered the hallway. Bird appeared at his cell like clockwork. Her beauty making that cold, hard, ugly, blue uniform look warm and sexy, but her tone wasn't so sweet.

"What's the matter?" he whispered

She turned her head trying to avoid eye contact.

"State your number Pipin."

He reached out and tried to touch her. She pulled back.

"State your number Pipin."

"429288"

"Thank you Pipin."

She walked away from his cell leaving him confused. It bothered him all day. When it was time for recreation, Evans came to his cell.

"Pipin, are you going to rec today?" She asked avoiding eye contact.

"No CO, I'm not. I need to talk. What's wrong?"

She looked at him and could barely hold back the tears.

"Trina, get me out of here so we can talk."

They went to their favorite spot. She told him about Sweany and her big argument. Sweany accused her of lying to him about money that was missing and of cheating. He threatened her.

"I want to end the relationship with him."

Dorel took her into his arms and she cried to him.

"Bird, stop crying. Does he know about us?"

"He doesn't."

"Trina, are you fucking with someone else?"

"No, Dorel how could you ask me something like that. I'm in love with you."

"What did you just say?"

"I said I love you."

"Trina, where is this coming from? A few months ago you told me that you loved Sweany."

"I did, but ever since I've been with you I don't want to be with him anymore. I don't want him to touch me. Dorel, I think about you all night when I'm not here."

"My beautiful bird, love is a strong word."

"I love you."

"I'm pregnant!"

Dorel looked at Trina like she just told him that he had one hour to live.

"Pregnant! Whose baby is it?"

"I'm sure it's yours."

"How do you know that it's not Sweany's?"

"Sweany and I haven't had sex in months. I'm sure it's yours."

"Bird what happened? Everything was perfect and in one day you come in here dropping bombs on my whole world."

"Your world? What about mine? My whole life is turned upside down."

"If Sweany finds out that you're pregnant by an inmate, he'll…?"

"No, no one knows except you and me."

"Good keep it that way. I'm going to call my people and they're going to arrange for you to move. I've one year left and when I come home we gonna be together. I need for you to lay low and don't tell anyone about the pregnancy. Stay away from Sweany as much as possible but don't act obvious. Just give me a few days and I'll have all this worked out."

"Sweany wants me to go to a Security convention in California."

"You can't go. Tell him that you are sick or something. Don't let him take you away from here. The weekend will be a perfect time for you to pack and leave town without him knowing anything while he's away. I'll have a place for you to go."

"Dorel, I love you. All I want is for us to be together with our baby. I'll do whatever."

"Listen, be very careful."

Later on that day Dorel went to the phones. That evening, he barely dozed off when his cell door was opened.

"Up on you feet Pipin."

"What's this, why…?"

"Shake-down, you know the routine."

"Pipin, you best shut your fucking mouth and stand to the side while my officers search your cell. Or, I'll have your ass carried off to the hole," Captain Sweany said as he walked into Dorel's cell.

Dorel wanted to kill Sweany especially knowing what he was doing to his bird. He gave Sweany the look of unmistakable hatred and revenge. He knew that one day he would be out there and would make Sweany pay.

Monday morning came and Dorel could hardly wait to hear the familiar phrase. It came but it wasn't that sweet, soft chirping he expected. Dorel went to the front of his cell to see CO Franklin. Where was Trina? He wondered.

Standing behind him was Sweany's six foot five frame.

"What's the problem Pipin? You look like you've lost something."

"Matter of fact I have. Someone's going to pay if I don't find it."

"Tough talk. Maybe you need time in the hole to cool you off. Then again you should be around the rest of the animals. They've a way of taking care of their own kind. Hey caged animal, your beautiful bird has been sprung," Sweany shouted over his broad shoulders in a matter-of-fact manner.

Dorel could hear the laughter rising above the sound of the buzzer. Sweany noisily walked away. He was left wondering about his bird. Dorel felt the sharp pain in his side. He looked at the blood on the shank in the fist of Hector, rat-killer. Hector lunged trying to wedge the make-shift knife into Dorel's mid-section. With the grace of a trained fighter, Dorel elbowed Hector, smashing his nose-bone. Hector fell and Dorel used Hector's hand with the shank to stab him in the neck.

Dazed, Dorel watched blood spurting out of the artery. The would-be assassin went into the throes of death's dance. The alarm went off, shutting down the facility. Guards charged from every direction. Dorel felt the blows to his head and everything went black.

It was a miracle. He felt her wings over him guiding him to the bright light. His bird was the answer to his prayers. It was freedom at last. The warmth of her smile melted his heart. No longer would they need to hide their love. His bird would shelter him from all coming storms. A smile creased his lips and Dorel drifted towards the light.

immersion
April Stokes

"I won't leave," he said.

When he first made love to her, he had understood that what he said was a lie. On some level he thought that she too knew this...Knew this lie. He thought that she understood that a promise is only as good as the moment it is spoken in. When he did leave, he saw the tears in her eyes.

"Don't go- you promised," he heard her say.

She knew that he never really meant it. After all, he was his father's son.

They said he'd be just like his father. They said, someday he'd let everyone down?

He hadn't tried hard to be like daddy, in fact, he had made no attempt at all.

It was an irrefutable fact. He was destined to be like that foul smelling, woman beating, drug sniffing, non-child support payin', m'f'er that had first deceived his momma and conceived him with the same lie.

"If you give me some, I promise I won't leave you."

In the end they had both left.

"You got your daddy's eyes."

When she first met Aurie Wright, he disgusted her. A tall, wiry man with no shirt and dirty, frayed jeans. He was repulsive, sitting on a dingy plastic chair. From his covered porch, Aurie watched the children playing, legs splayed before him, hair wildly plaited coming undone. He was a sturdy man, muscular man. No more than twenty-five the glow of youth was fading. He barely looked at her when she walked up the stairs of his front porch. Her first impression of him was fear.

"Hello, I'm here to see Mr. Wright," she said standing in front of him.

"A pleasure," he smiled with too much tooth. Without saying anything else, he sat watching her in the blazing, Atlanta afternoon sun. She was already upset because she must have been the only person working on the day before the 4th of July.

On top of that, this asshole was just sitting there staring at her. When Sydney first knew that she would have to work with him, she protested to her boss. She didn't want to make the hour long drive to his shabby house. Sydney didn't want to do the token black story; disenfranchised youth making ghetto mosaics. Knowing for sure that this was a waste of her time, Sydney fought to stay away from places like this. She suspected the substandard art he produced would not be worth her time. He was surprisingly soft-spoken and educated, having dropped out twenty-eight credits from a degree in psychology.

She shifted her weight wishing that she wasn't wearing four inch-stilettos. Finally, he sat up stiffly from his chair like a man twice his age, gave a lengthy stretch and yawn and waved her through the opening to his home.

They moved through the small doorway into Aurie's home. She was disappointed to feel that the temperature was no better inside. It was suffocating. A gloss of sweat formed on her forehead as they entered what she guessed was a living room. There was a card table and two folding chairs in the center of the room. A tattered brown sofa was in front of the mantle. It reminded her of her own childhood and she felt sadness. Along the mantle were several photos of people having fun. The pictures seemed out of place. Almost out of sight was a black and white photo with fading faces. Directly across from the window was a tall wooden bookcase that looked old and weathered.

Aurie led her through the swinging doors and gracefully ushered her into the kitchen. She felt a rush of cool air. The room was small and cramped. Sitting on the windowsill, a noisy air conditioner blew cool air. The walls were the color of split peas. The cupboards were painted the same shade of green. The whole room was beyond repair. Sydney held back a gag when she saw the rolling cart loaded with jars and jars of pickled pig feet and snouts.

Aurie squeezed around the table to reveal the thing that she had come to see. There, leaning against the wall, behind an old sheet, was a large square glass mirror. The frame was covered in the most beautiful glass mosaic she had ever seen. She felt drawn to it. Aurie pulled the curtain over the air conditioner. When the light penetrated the glass, it echoed and danced.

"It's beautiful." Sydney gasped loudly and a smile formed on her glossed lips. She moved close to Aurie and could hear his hurried breathing. Her career as an art journalist was reduced to second-rate articles no one remembered. Dreams seemed far out of reach. Her mind began to click.

"What is it? I mean what do you use to create the pieces?" She asked, the man taking new shape in her eyes.

"Broken bits of things, glass, sometimes metal. I use the leftover pieces of people's lives and put 'em back together." He shrugged. "The trick of it is time. Time and patience," he said in a slow drawl. He was right. The detail and intricacy of his work must take hours to create.

"None of 'em is the same. Each is different. It's like the glass is alive and they take the shape thar born ta be."

The words came out sounding rehearsed like something he'd read from one of the art magazines he had carefully placed on the kitchen table. He appeared not to take notice or care of the world around him yet he tried to impress her.

"Where shall we begin?" She said taking a seat.

"It's up to you Miss Lady. I'm here ta please." There was that grin again. The more she saw it the more he began to look like a sheepish little boy. She didn't want to stay long and had called a day earlier in preparation for the visit. She remembered calling him. The phone rang several times before he answered sleepily.

"Hello?"

"Mr. Wright? I'm sorry if I woke you. This is Sydney Graham from *Mode*. You received our letter?" What was he doing sleeping in the middle of the afternoon?

"Yeah, yeah I got it. Some sort of art story right?" She sighed heavily with impatience. He had no idea what was going on. He probably didn't even know what art was. Just some back hills bumpkin who happened on something pretty.

"Yes, it's a story."

"Each year our magazine features up and coming artists. You and your work have been selected to be part of this issue. There are a lot of people who find your story and your work very fascinating. Our publication, *Mode,* is well known in both commercial and academic circles. You should be proud." She had fed him the required bullshit.

The conversation was forced and labored. Getting her point across in a way that she thought he could understand was like pulling teeth. In the end, they had agreed to meet at his home. She had cleared her calendar for this day.

Driving across town and back took a chunk of it. Sydney wore her favorite black Armani pantsuit. This morning in the mirror she saw the twenty pounds she had gained staring angrily back at her. She had dieted feverishly to leave them but the resolute pounds stayed. Her favorite suit made her feel better. Sparkling costume jewels studded her ears and looped her neck.

Sydney touched her earring as Aurie sat at the table across from her, self-conscious that he might see through her façade.

"Tell me your story," she said.

He took a breath as though he had prepared all night for this moment. Then he rubbed his toffee colored hands together. They were big as oars and rough looking. She watched him not really listening at first. As he continued to speak she was drawn in by the tragedy of his story.

The editor of Sydney's magazine stumbled across it one day while looking for antiques in the countryside. She had wandered into a small, cluttered second-hand shop where an old woman greeted her. It was the impetus for the follow-up on Aurie's story. The old woman had reminded her of grandma.

Most of the items in the shop were of little importance and were covered with dust. She was in a sneezing frenzy when something in the corner of a long glass case caught her eye. It could've been just another glass picture frame, so delicate she thought she might break it. She bought it for five dollars and an hour later, Sydney's editor emerged from the shop with damp eyes and an intense fervor to find Aurie Wright.

He was born in the late 70's to a woman whose name he barely remembered. His mother was a pretty girl with sad eyes. He never knew where she came from or who his people were. He had known that he had a daddy for biological reasons, but who that man was his mother would never say. They were poor, but Aurie didn't know it. Not because his mother filled the void in other ways, but because all the other kids in the neighborhood were just as poor. None of them had fathers that stayed, so he figured he wasn't at too much of a disadvantage.

His mother went out a lot. She wasn't the type for PTA and seemed overly disappointed with her life. And as though she were trying to save the remaining deficient pieces, she gathered her things in two plastic trash bags and walked out of the house that she and Aurie shared. She left two dollars and a tattered picture of young Mary and baby Jesus. The back of it was signed: *Love mommy.*

This haunted Aurie. He feared that maybe his mother was looking for him. Social workers found him three months later- dirty with his ribs poking through his skin. They forced him to leave the house. He had nightmares that his mother was there, waiting for him to come home. She never returned.

He found himself in foster care until he settled with an older Baptist Minister and his wife. The couple adopted young Aurie and gave him their name. He was happy with them for a time. They were not particularly strict and gave Aurie everything he wanted and needed. Aurie's own broken pieces seemed to come together.

When he was fifteen, the cruel fabric of life began to tear again. He and his parents were coming home from a revival which had lasted from Friday to Sunday evening. Though the revival was three hours away and Mrs. Wright had begged him to wait until morning, Reverend Wright insisted on leaving right after the lengthy service.

Reluctantly, Mrs. Wright piled into the car. They began the journey talking. Aurie remembered yielding to his dreams as the Reverend hummed: How Great Thou Art. The old Buick sped along Highway 85. Aurie awoke two days later with his tongue thick. He was extremely thirsty and confused.

Aurie expected to be at home but the white room around him was not his own. The light was so bright his head throb and threw him into a desperate panic. A nurse came and quieted him with a glass of water and codeine. Aurie felt the familiar sting of loss creeping over him.

It happened two nights ago as Aurie slept soundly in the back seat of the Buick and Mrs. Wright dozed in the front. Reverend Wright nodded off and awoke too late to avoid the strong oak that stood unmoved when their car plowed head-on into it. They were just five miles from home. Mrs. Wright was killed instantly. Reverend Wright held on for thirty minutes after his body was tossed and crushed easily as a flower.

"I'm so sorry Jesus. I'm so sorry." He was uttering to the paramedics who found him twelve feet away from the car. Except for a badly broken leg, Aurie was alive. He escaped with a slight limp and was parentless again. In his anger, he turned away from the Jesus who he had learned loved him.

With nowhere else to go, he was placed in a group home where he grew increasingly withdrawn. He met a young counselor, Melinda, who worked part-time in the evenings. She was not much older and took to him immediately. She would sit with him showing him art books and reading him poetry. One evening, while everyone slept, Melinda led Aurie to the river behind the house. They dipped their toes in the chilly water and skipped rocks. The place became a secret hangout.

Aurie had made his first glass piece for Melinda, from a frame he found in the trash and broken pieces of stained glass he found near a church. That night he presented it to her. She gazed at it and wept. Aurie put his lips to her cheek tasting her tears. Telling him that he was sweet, she did not protest as he undid the buttons of her shirt. In the solitude of the river, they made love.

She hadn't felt dirty afterward or even ashamed though she knew somehow it was wrong. Aurie was still only a boy but he loved her like no man had. For three months the secret carried on between the two of them. Silently, fervently like a fire burning in a room of matches. Her husband found out and blacked both her eyes. He knocked a hole in her mouth where teeth once were.

While nursing his swollen knuckles she held the Glock 28 semi-automatic to her temple and ended her life. The grief broke Aurie.

"I used to tell stories in the beginning, you know, just to sell the pieces," he looked away from Sydney, ashamed.

"Stories…?"

"Yeah you know. Lies, seemed like folks liked the made up stories better. Folks who didn't know me that is."

"But it didn't seem right. It just didn't."

She held his hand. Looking at him intently, his sadness touched her. It wasn't hard to see that Aurie was wounded. She'd have to tread carefully to get what she wanted.

Sydney pulled off from the curb in her polished, luxury car. She watched Aurie through her rearview window. He stood both happy and sad, house falling down around him. Even though he was repugnant, Aurie was a marvel. He was unmatched in his field of art. His work had made Aurie Wright a lone flower in a field of crab grass.

She made an unscheduled visit the next time. Sydney drove the long hour only to sit in the car thinking, waiting, plotting. Aurie walked to the car, before she had even noticed he was coming. He knocked at the passenger side and motioned for her to roll down the window.

"Come inside. You'll burn up out here. An' I got ice-tea for you."

He smiled and turned back to the house. Aurie made it easy for her. No excuses necessary. She put her keys in her purse, grabbed her tape recorder and followed him into the house. This would be easier than she thought.

They sat in the living room, feeling the evening summer breeze through the open window. Sydney sipped her tea slowly, deliberately. She knew that he was watching her and it was delicious. She began to wonder what else he mastered.

"You want answers right? You're wondering *why*," he finally said. Without saying anything she had given herself away.

"Yes Aurie, I need answers. I need to understand your gift."

She heard him laughing.

"You can't understand a gift. It ain't taught. Why me? I don't know, don't care. But that piece thar on the wall. That's me and nobody can take that."

His words rang true to her. She stared at him as he sat next to her. After a moment he got up from the sofa and moved to the kitchen. He came back with an odd shaped object wrapped in newspaper and tied with string.

"Here," he said, holding the gift towards her, like an

offering. "I made it for you. Hope you like it."

She hastily tore at the paper. He had given her the only thing that he possessed. The small gift of glass was just the right encouragement she needed. She felt a twinge of jealously for the woman who had risked everything to love him.

"You touch me," she said placing the gift on the table. The moment was awkward because Sydney knew she was going to make something happen. It made her tingle. The expectation caused a sensation she hadn't felt and the anticipation of something new was enticing.

She tenderly kissed him with her eyes open, then again eagerly. Sydney felt his desire, he wanted it. She watched him, tasting his mouth completely this time. He caressed her head and neck with gentleness, laid her back and removed her blouse. Her chest heaved as he found his way down her torso, stopping to nibble at her breasts, her belly, then going further finding her center and treating it like a toy chest. She let him take her on the soiled couch that smelled of beer and cheap cigars.

A small price to pay for success, she hardly noticed the springs digging into her back. It amused her that when he climaxed a shiver ran across his body. He held her close when it subsided, as though afraid to let go.

"I knew you were good," she sighed.

Sydney seduced him on the couch and her plan was in effect. While they lay there breathing, she thought of all the ways she could ride him. Love or sex was not her care, only money and the insane accrual of it.

It didn't take long for Aurie to make good on her investment. She poured her heart into his career, becoming his exclusive voice to the masses and taking on the burden of managing his swelling fortune. She encouraged him and convinced him that it was all for love; his love of art, her love of him.

The Yuppies had a weakness for him and Black folks thought he was the voice of the broken. He was the perfect mascot. It became easier for her to want him, knowing that everyone wanted a piece of him and she had him turned her on. Aurie was ever grateful. He allowed her to fix his teeth, his hair now combed and braided in wonderfully precise lines that reminded her of perfect rows of corn when she rubbed his head. He was ravenous with her body. She let him take her every kinky way possible. He wanted to fuck with the lights on, wanted her to take it from behind, and any other hole where he could fit. She just groaned with satisfaction, thinking only of the things he brought her.

Sydney supposed that they were both happy with the arrangement. She was surprised to see him one afternoon, walking casually with another woman's hand clinging to his. She watched them, stalked them. Sydney saw that the eyes of the woman were intent on Aurie as though *she* possessed him.

She had remarkable control when it came to revenge. Sydney watched with a cold, detached vision of her world unraveling like a cheap sweater. She looked at every inch of the woman. Noticed her hair, her nails, her clothes, she and the woman were nothing alike. She watched Aurie kissing the new woman, like he had kissed her. She wondered where else he had kissed the woman.

Sydney was amazed at how furtive she could be. If she were not in the situation herself, she may have gloated in the sheer genius of her efforts. Before entering Aurie's house a voice should've gone off in her head. She had long since turned off the part of her brain that listened to reason. Aurie left the woman alone in the house.

She had sneaked to a local locksmith and had made a copy of his keys since he had first bought his new home in Buckhead.

When Sydney had first seen the woman with Aurie, she felt rage and hatred of an angry wife. She had only been with him for the fortune, but had been good to him. Sydney passed through the kitchen and into the great room, she smirked thinking that the dumb bitch hadn't even set the alarm. Probably didn't know the code. She heard the TV upstairs and followed the sound.

Whatever courage she lacked when she walked up the stairs, she found as she turned the corner to the master suite. Sydney saw the woman lying casually across *her* man's bed.

"Who the fuck are *you*?" She asked trying to remain calm.

"I know you," the woman said. "Why are you here?"

The pistol came out then. Sydney pulled it from under her shirt. The very thing she had sworn she wouldn't use. She meant to scare the little man-stealing whore. For a moment, she thought that a divine presence would intervene and stop her from doing the crazy-ass white slut. Sydney held the trigger a few seconds longer in anticipation of God Almighty stepping into the bedroom where she had passionately called His name. Her eyes twitched and she licked her lips just before she squeezed. Only one shot, no, bitch was going to take what was hers.

"I'm losing my mind. I'm losing my *fucking* mind."

The horror on the woman's face pleased Sydney, yet she felt numb. There was no remorse. Something unexpected happened then. The tables turned and all of her calculations on his life had not factored in this moment. Aurie walked in.

"Hello Sydney. Ya know, when I met you, I knew thar was something 'bout you. I *just* couldn't put my finger on it. Then I had it, most niggas wish they had my passion. Wish they could feel it for something, anything. You wanted it everyday of yo' boring ass life. You put on yer suits to feel powerful and real. You see all this round you. This *my* shit! I made this. I made *you!* You use people; that's the only way you can git what you want. So you should really appreciate *this…* This here is my fiancée, Melinda."

Sydney's eyes went from Aurie to the bitch and back to Aurie. Pity, she had only had one round left.

"Son of a Bitch," she whispered.

Aurie saw when she walked to the house. He remembered it because it was the day before the 4th of July and the kids were running crazy in the streets. Shit, he had seen the wide body Benz coming down the block and had known it was her. He smelled her perfume as she sidled toward him from the car in her Armani suit and cubic zirconium bling. He glanced at her and saw her eyes watching him, sizing him up. She had an attitude that he wanted to conquer and he knew one thing, he would have her. That art shit was just icing on the cake.

greed
Kiniesha Gayle

Prologue

CLING!

The sound of iron bars could be heard slamming throughout the prison. Once I was inside my cell, the handcuffs and shackles were taken off. I gently rubbed my wrist and glanced around the dank, lonely cell. The reality that I was about to die finally kicked in. I made my way over to the iron bed with a thin mattress and grey blanket. Leaning against the cold wall, I sat with my knees to my chest.

If only I could turn back the hands of time, I thought and

rolled my eyes to the ceiling. Officer Gamby, a slender man with straight black hair, pulled up a chair next to my cell. Our eyes made contact. His eyes told a story that was surely impossible to figure out in the next twenty-four hours.

June nineteenth was the day I was sentenced to die by lethal injection. My life slowly replayed before my watery eyes. I was crying, something I hadn't done many years now. The judge or lawyers didn't see my tears. Here as I let it flow, Officer Gamby saw my tears.

"Are you alright?" he asked passing me tissues.

I took them, paused and a chuckle escaped my lip.

"If I did the crime, the fact that I didn't do it doesn't make me feel so good. I was framed by a system that was supposed to protect me."

"That's kinda hard to prove."

He walked back over to where he was seated before continuing.

"If I could get a dollar for each time an inmate on death row states that they're innocent, I'll be a rich man by now."

I got up off the bed, walked over to the steel bars next to Officer Gamby.

"There's a difference between me and them, I'm telling

the truth," I said staring at him.

"If you say so," he said nonchalantly and crossed his leg.

Summer 94

My heart pounded as I quickly made my way through Philadelphia's Penn Station. I checked the ticket. The train to New York City was leaving in forty-five minutes. I looked around trying to be inconspicuous. The more I stood around the more nervous I became.

I pulled the brim of my Stetson down and headed for the coffee shop. My eyes searched the area for any hint of the police following me.

I can't wait to get to New York and escape all this madness, I thought sipping the java brew. The Louis Vuitton traveling bag which contained the money was tucked under my arm.

I sat down in a corner where no one could see me. That seating allowed me to see everything in view. I even watched television to catch up on the latest news.

Commuters quickly crowded the station's platform. Silently, I watched them scramble to get to work. My thoughts were put on full blast when I heard the news on the radio.

...In other news headline: Police are still trying to find the killer of millionaire tycoon Nick Riggs. Mr. Riggs was found dead in his Philadelphia mansion late last night. Police have no lead, and Mr. Riggs's wife is missing...

"Aw fuck!" I muttered under my breath. The hot coffee splashed on my thigh as I hurriedly grabbed my bag and headed for the exit. I heard the announcement.

"10:30 Train to New York City now boarding at gate 10..."

I quickly made my way to the gate and handed the conductor my ticket.

"Do you have any ID?" A short, stocky man with white beard asked.

"ID?" I questioned.

"Yes, for security reasons."

I wanted to curse his white ass out, but instead I held my composure and handed him my ID. The clerk scrutinized it, looked up at me, and began to pull out his radio.

Oh shit! I must get out of here. I'm going to jail. I can't go to jail. Sweat poured down my back as I began to panic.

"Is there a problem?" I asked trying to sound calm.

"No, not all. I was just admiring your beauty."

My insides boiled with rage. I grabbed my ID and went down the steps to board the train. I found my seat, placed the bag in the corner next to me and placed my feet on it. I reached for my CD player and allowed Whitney Houston to seep into my ears. A sigh of relief escaped before I closed my eyes for the two hour train ride.

1986

"C'mon, you're making us late," father yelled.

"Be safe, and remember I love you."

Mother kissed me on the cheek. This was the last time she would see me. Tears rolled down her face and my ten year old face. The thought of leaving her for good was overwhelming to both of us. My father, whom I only saw once before this, convinced my mother that America would be better for me. Mother was poor and agreed. She promised to join me later.

"Listen there's no time for this fucking shit." Father was irritated.

"You're taking my only daughter from me," my mother said.

"No, please don't let me go mama." I screamed as he lifted me up and threw me in the car. Tears rolling, I looked at my mother who knelt in the dirt crying her heart out. There was confusion in my mind. I couldn't understand why my father didn't take mother with us.

The journey to Norman Manley International Airport in Kingston, Jamaica got off to a bumpy start. I leaned my head on the back of the seat and cried myself to sleep.

I was later awakened by the sound of the flight attendant stating that we needed to fasten our seatbelts. Father sat next to me. Not once did we exchange words.

Four and half hours later the flight landed at JFK airport. A slight delay through customs and we were on our way to Creston Avenue in the Bronx.

There was graffiti all over the building. People were outside listening and dancing to the loud music of rap.

My mouth fell open and my eyes bugged out when we went into his apartment. Mother's home in Jamaica was small and very well kept. Here in New York, I saw dirty clothes on the floor and dirty dishes on the dining table. Flies were everywhere and there was this horrible stench.

"Is this where we're going to live?' I asked trying to hold

my breath.

"Yes, get comfortable." His tone was nastier than before.

There was a dark skin lady with short hair and big gold earrings in her ears lying across an unmade bed. My father walked over to her and kissed her. I sat on a chair in the hallway as questions bombarded my mind.

"Hi Nicole, I'm Lisa. Your father's told me all about you."

Her smile left me wondering about health plans and dental services. She appeared frail and unhealthy. I smiled without opening my mouth and walked away.

Last day of class

The school bell rang ending the school year. Going to school was the best part of my life. It offered a chance to escape the madness surrounding me. My father's girlfriend was seriously working on my last nerves. We were living in the middle of the crack epidemic. I knew that the bitch was using crack. I couldn't understand what father saw in her.

Since arriving, I hadn't spoken to mother. I wrote to

her twice weekly. Approaching the building, I spotted the EMS carrying someone out on a stretcher covered in a black bag. It was none of my business but I stared for a second then continued upstairs. My main focus was to get a good job and go live on my own. At the entrance to my apartment, I saw a police officer, and there were people taking photos. I saw my father sitting down on a chair looking the worse I've seen him. A bottle of Gin sat open on the table.

"What's wrong?" I asked walking to him. Never had I shown love to him, but something in his eyes told me he needed it. I rubbed his shoulder.

"Lisa's dead," he stated before letting out a loud cry.

"How, what happened?" I asked.

He turned his head and stared.

"Go in the living room."

It wasn't a good time to challenge him. I obeyed and took a seat in the living room. I turned on the TV.

Days turned into weeks and father wasn't getting any better. He would stroll in late at night smelling like alcohol and funk. He started sleeping days and missing work. The bills began piling up.

"Nicole," he called from his bedroom. Sweat poured off

his body. He was standing in his underpants. My father had lost a lot of weight.

"I need you to be dressed early tomorrow morning. I need help around here with the bills. I spoke with my boss and he said you can come to work."

"What about school?" I protested.

"That'll have to be put on hold. Classes don't put food on the table or clothing on your back. The bills need to be paid, and you need to get a job to help around here."

"Yes sir," I walked away hissing.

The next day I was on my way to Scarsdale N.Y. to work with the Riggs family.

Torture

"Take this dick." Mr. Riggs grunted thrusting in and out of me.

He was sweating like there was no tomorrow. My legs were upright in the air and tears were flowing. I closed my eyes wondering why my father sold me into this. Two years ago he died from an overdose of crack. He also had the virus.

After his death, I had nowhere to go. The Riggs' decided

to take me in. I sure did pay a hell of a price to live there. Four nights a week Mr. Riggs would be fucking the shit out of me. He took my virginity and got me pregnant three times. I was forced to have an abortion each time. This time I outsmarted him. I was given birth control pills by the clinic and ever since then I've been on them. Mr. Riggs body shook and I knew he was about to ejaculate.

When he was finished, he got up, wiped his little, pink, limp-dick. Told me he would see me in another two nights and crept back to bed with his wife.

I'd cry after he left my room. I had no one to console me or understand what I was going through. There was a knock on the door.

"Are you okay?" Mr. Riggs' son opened the door and came in.

"Yeah," I said wiping my eyes.

"Okay either you're a good actress or you lying. Because no one cries so much until their pillow's soaked." He reached over and felt my pillow.

A smile creased my lips, something I hadn't done in a long time.

"Are you going to talk to me?" He asked.

"I'm sad and I've got no one to talk to."

I didn't get into too much detail because some things were best kept in the dark.

Time went on and we became extremely close. Two years later Nick Riggs moved out and took me along with him. Neither his father nor mother was pleased. They threatened to disown him if he left with me. We did and continued on with our relationship.

"I still don't get how you ended up on death row?" Officer Gamby asked interrupting my story.

"I'm almost there." I said cutting him off.

Nick had just received a promotion and became president for the advertisement firm where he worked. The promotion required that we relocate. We decided to splurge and buy a two-million dollar house in Pennsylvania. Nick and I were all set to withdraw four million dollars from the bank. Two million was for the home another million for decorations. The other mill was for starting my own fashion business. With all this money coming from his account, word got back to the older Riggs. I remembered the day before picking up the money I got a telephone call from Nick.

"You lying bitch, how could you?" he yelled through the phone.

"What are you talking about?" I asked.

"You slept with my father and got pregnant by him three times, and then had three different abortions?" His anger seeped.

"I'm sorry. Let me explain." I began crying.

"It's a little too late, honey. I want you out of my house before I return in the next two days. I'll be removing your name from the bank accounts and life insurance."

"So Nick took out a life insurance policy with your name on it?" Gamby once again interrupted as he now sat upright to get the rest of the story. "How much was it worth?" He leaned closer to the bars.

"Couple million dollars," I answered.

Gamby's eyes popped wide open as he repeated like an echo, "Millions? I see why you on death row."

"Anyway," I said brushing his comment aside. "Do you want me to continue or not?"

"Yeah go ahead." He said eyeing me and leaning back.

My anger peaked. Not only did he make war between me and my husband, but my husband was now getting ready to file for divorce. The following day I went to the gun shop and purchased a .22 caliber shotgun. I couldn't bear losing my best friend, my husband. I decided that I was going to take the four million dollars since Nick had already placed his signature on the card. I was going to New York to kill Mr. Riggs and his wife, and then try to plead with Nick. If he wouldn't listen to what I had to say, I would kill him and shoot myself. Then make it look like a break in. I had it all planned.

I met with this hit man to do the job. I was too chicken-shit to do the job myself. He wanted fifty thousand for both murders. I paid him half the money and the other half was to be paid when the job was complete. The following day I got a call from the hit-man asking if we could meet for lunch. When I got there he had information for me. The good news was that Riggs and his family had been murdered. The bad news was he hadn't pulled the trigger. He found them dead upon breaking into the home.

I left and immediately boarded a flight back to Philly to meet up with my husband to see if things could be worked out. When I opened the door, I found my husband slumped over the sofa, hands bound behind his back. He had been shot in the head, execution style.

"Okay now this is becoming weirder by the moment." Gamby said pulling his chair closer to the cell. "How did you end up in prison?"

The news flash ripped through Philadelphia and NYC like a heat wave. When I got off the Amtrak train, I was greeted by my cousin, and two plainclothes detectives.

"I'm sorry the reward was too great." My cousin said.

They found my prints on the door, the gun that I purchased

had prints on it. It was the gun that was used to kill my Nick.

"If you didn't kill them, then who do you think...?" Gamby leaned forward in the chair and asked.

"I don't know," I said gripping the bars.

"I never believed inmates when they tell me their story, but for some reason I believe you."

I was given my last meal and was pondering all the things I could have done right. It was too late for that. After I finished this meal I'll be walking to the death chamber.

"Do you want to see a priest or a reverend?"

I shook my head.

"We got one standing by, just in case." I was told then strapped to a gurney.

There were a bevy of people around me including doctors and officers. I saw the closed curtain. Then it slowly opened and I saw faces. None I knew and didn't care to know.

"Any last words, Miss?"

"I'm innocent."

My arm was set in place and the IV needle attached then inserted into my arm. The phone sounded loudly as it rang. It was the governor. I had been granted a stay.

Epilogue

Warm sun rays caressed my back. I stood on the balcony of my San Diego home. The smell of coffee lingered. I tied the string of my white robe, and read the newspaper. I was due to go shopping in another hour. I was waiting for my girlfriend, Tiffany to stop by.

The governor stayed my execution and I was able to win my freedom because the blood at the crime scene didn't match my own. When they checked the hotel records at the time of the murder, they saw that I was in my room. I wasn't a murderer.

"Oh well all that ends well, is definitely well for me."

You see the trick to this was, I hired a hit-man to kill the Riggs but knew later on he would snitch. So I hired professionals. I used one and half million to hire a detective from the force of thirty years to carry out the killing. The other million was paid to a forensic scientist who helped to contaminate the crime scene. I allowed the hit-man to go there and see the bodies because that way he wouldn't have a guilty conscience. He didn't commit the murders, he got paid for the job as if he did it, and he was living comfortable.

Nick? He had to die because he had too many connections

in high places. He would've hunted his father's killers. I couldn't stand losing the millions in the account and this life insurance. As for my time in jail, some things have to be staged in order to make it look real.

"Such a nice day outside," Tiffany said kissing me hard.

"Heard from your father lately?" I smiled returning her kiss.

"You mean the governor?"

We hugged, laughed and walked into the sunlight.

biographies

Genieva Borne is a single mother of two who once lived in Baltimore, Maryland. Ms. Borne resides in New York City where she attends college. She credits Alice Walker's *The Color Purple* as the book that had the most influence on her. "Writing is liberation from the hardship that comes with life. I hope other people are able to relate to what the characters are going through in my stories."

Sharron Doyle is a hardworking writer from New York City. She wrote four titles while incarcerated. Her debut titled, *If It Ain't One Thing It's Another*, hit stores fall 06. Sharron stays busy in Harlem searching to write the perfect novel. Trini is her nickname. Ms. Doyle is proud of her Trinidad and Tobago roots. She lists her mother as a strong influence in her life. "I feel like I can take it to any level I want to, when I'm on top of my writing game."

Kineisha Gayle was born in Kingston, Jamaica. She earned a BA in Forensic Psychology at John Jay College of Criminal Justice. "I developed a passion for writing at nine years old. I started out writing poetries and short stories." In 02 she completed *King of Spades,* her first manuscript. The novel sold very well. "Writing is a major part of my life." *Deadly Freaks & Queen of Hearts* are her upcoming titles.

Joy Leftow grew up in Washington Heights. Since the early nineties, Joy has been hitting the NYC poetry scene with her unique prose style. *A Spot Of Bleach & Other Poems and Prose* (05, Big Foot Press) is her current release. Joy holds a BA and MSW from Columbia University. *Some folks accuse me of being post modernist…others say my prose depicts the harder and sharper sides. My ability is mitzvah. It's my love…the finished product, the offspring.*

Princess Madison was bitten by the writing bug after she read *Ghetto Falsehoods,* a novel by Anthony Whyte. "Truthfully, I thought I could write and had dabbled. After reading the novel, I analyzed the characters and the story. It really stirred and influenced me." Princess Madison's debut title *Gangster Bitch,* is due fall 08.

Vanessa Martir grew up in Bushwick, Brooklyn. Her journals became her escape while coping with the shock of leaving New York at the age of thirteen. Vanessa studied and lived at Wellesley, MA. A graduate of Columbia University in NY, Vanessa completed her first novel after the birth of her daughter. The hot debut, *Woman's Cry ~Llanto de la Mujer,* is due fall 06. "I want to do spoken word again. Anais Nin said, *'To write is to taste life twice. '"*

Justice Mejia was born in New York City. She currently resides in Brooklyn. She wrote her first poem *Rainbow* at age eight. "I think the way words are used is art. They can make you feel, cry, laugh, or even open your mind to another world." Justice is inspired by Emily Dickinson, Zane, Robert Frost and most importantly life. "I think life is already written; we can at times adjust the words but the outcome remains the same."

Tri Smith's signature is the unexpected twist. She is the author of adult best-sizzlers: *They Call Me Miss Divine* and *The Bristol Ho-tel I & II*. Ms. Smith is a professional magazine and book editor, and feature writer. Published poet (Blind Beggar Press) and spoken word performer (Aretha Franklin Award 2005). She is working on the completion of her fourth novel, an intriguing murder mystery. Read free chapters of her erotic fiction and order copies at www.trismithbooks.com.

April D. Stokes was born in Pittsburgh, PA where she began writing poetry and short stories at the age of 7. She attended Cornell University where she received her Bachelors degree and has continued to pursue her love of writing. She currently lives in Atlanta, GA and enjoys swimming, traveling and art. She is currently working on her first novel which is a continuation of the story: *Immersion*.

Leah Whitney writes and edits from Queens, NY. "My need to fix the document spurred me into the field of editing." A graduate of Pace University, Leah is influenced by Zora Neale Hurston, James Baldwin and Toni Morrison. Leah is the editor of novels such as *Road Dawgz* by K'wan, *Blinded* by Kashamba Williams, *A Hood Legend* and its sequel, *Menage's Way*, both by Victor L. Martin, *Booty Call *69,* by Erick S. Gray and *If It Ain't One Thing It's Another*, by Sharron Doyle.

Crystal Lacey Winslow is a Brooklyn-born author who began writing creatively at an early age. Her unique storytelling technique is evident in her deeply personal spoken word/poetry book Melodrama, and her character-driven and remarkably visual novel *Life, Love & Loneliness.* Crystal earned her baccalaureate degree in Legal Assistant Studies. She started Melodrama Publishing in 2001. *The Criss Cross, Wifey, Still Wifey* and *Menace To Society,* are some recent titles.

Special thanks to the Augustus Manuscript Team aka the Dream Team: JayClay, Tamiko Maldonado, Sofia Urena. Thanks L. Hyatt for the title suggestion.

Go hard or go home...

Llantó de la mujer

WOMAN'S *cry*

A NOVEL BY
VANESSA MÁRTIR

AUGUSTUS
PUBLISHING

5

"I'm not feelin' your man, bella," Anais said as she affectionately pushed my hair behind my ear. Her other hand was around my waist. "This is about me and you beautiful." She kissed my neck.

"But…" I hesitated and pulled away. I looked back to see if Fabian had parked the car. "He's my man. He's gonna wanna get down. I thought you understood that."

"I don't want to cause any friction between you and your man, boo, but I have to be real. I'm just not diggin' him like that. His whole vibe bothers me. It's hateful and vicious. I came because I want you. I need to feel you." She drew me close. "I want to please you in a way you can't imagine. He can watch if he wants but that's it." She wrapped her tongue around mine and made me forget about Fabian. Neither of us saw him approach.

"Can I have some of that?" Fabian grabbed both our asses roughly. Anais cringed and tried to hide her repugnance but the quickness of her withdrawal gave it away. Fabian looked at her perplexed but before he could say anything, I planted a wet kiss on his open mouth.

"Wanna play, pa?" I asked, caressing his crotch.

We went upstairs together with me walking deliberately in between Fabian and Anais. When we entered the apartment, I lit candles, put Sade's Greatest Hits on the surround sound, and served us all tall glasses of Grey Goose and cranberry. I excused myself and went into the bathroom where I prepared a bath of jasmine essence and rose petals in the Jacuzzi.

I could feel the tension in the living room when I reentered. I heard Anais's pleasant raspy voice singing along to Sade's Smooth Operator and looked over to see Fabian rolling a huge L of 'dro. Anais and Fabian sat on opposite sides of the butter leather coach, not looking at or speaking to one another. We puffed the blunt while Sade's silky voice sang in the background.

When we finished puffing, I led them both to the bathroom. I pecked Anais and sat her down on the edge of the hot tub. "I'll be with you in a moment," I said with a flirtatious smile. Before I could turn around, I heard Fabian swiftly unzip his pants, rip off his shirt, popping buttons in his haste, and splash into the hot tub.

Damn, talk about thirsty! *¡Que lambón!* I thought unamused, arching my eyebrows at his annoying over-eagerness. I looked over at Anais. Her expression revealed that she was thinking the exact same thing.

Fabian looked at us both with a huge grin, shrugged and asked, "Y'all joining me or what?"

"Now you gotta wait for us," I responded.

Anais and I slowly began to undress one another in between kisses to the lips, neck and breasts. Fabian bit his bottom lip as he watched. We stepped into the tub. To Fabian's surprise, I placed myself in between him and Anais. I remembered what Anais had said to me and could tell from her body language that Anais was serious about not getting down with Fabian. I hurriedly kissed Fabian and jerked him off trying to distract him while with my other hand, I discreetly stimulated Anais's clitoris. Anais grabbed the loofah, poured some Victoria's Secret Forbidden Fantasy body wash on it and began to gently scrub my shoulders and back.

Fabian stood up and rammed his rock hard penis into my mouth. I gagged and tried to pull back but he grabbed me by the nape of my neck and wouldn't let go. My eyes watered but I let him manhandle me. I knew that if I tried to stop him, he'd go into a rampage and would kick Anais out or worse, get violent with us both. I sucked him off until he came, which wasn't long because despite his constant bragging, the truth was he was a three minute man.

Fabian clenched my hair, forcing me to keep his eight inches deep in my throat until the last drop of cum spewed from his dick. When he was done, he carelessly got out of the tub. "I'll wait for y'all in the bedroom," he muttered without even a glance back. I hadn't noticed that Anais had stopped bathing me and was staring open mouthed in shock.

"What the fuck was that?" Her voice held a mixture of anger and sadness.

"That was nothing, ma." I tried to hide the sorrow. "Now he'll leave us alone for a while."

Anais looked at me forlornly and cradled me in her arms. We bathed one another and kissed for what seemed like forever. By the time we went to the bedroom, Fabian had fallen asleep on the chaise longue opposite the California king size bed. We were both relieved but neither said anything.

We fell onto the silk sheets into each other's arms. Anais grabbed me by the wrists and held them over my head rendering me motionless. She bit me gently but firmly on the lips and neck.

"There's velvet rope in the top drawer," I whispered, coyly motioning towards the night table. Anais slipped the smooth cord around my wrists and in between the brass headboard, making it a point to leave them loose enough so she wouldn't have trouble changing my position. She then proceeded to slowly and methodically lick and nibble me from head to toe.

I whimpered as Anais worked her way down my torso. She left no inch of my body untouched. When she reached my pussy, she licked my Brazilian waxed bikini line and stroked my clitoris but mischievously proceeded to kiss and bite around my crotch and on my inner thigh, not stopping until she reached the point of each toe. She then turned me around and did the same to my back.

I quivered and moaned uncontrollably when Anais reached the small of my back. This was one of my weak spots. I gasped in delight as she began to lick my ass and finger me from behind. Several times I felt like I was about to cum but just when I was about to reach the height, Anais withdrew and began to lick another spot and stimulate another area. I glanced at her, dizzy with rapture, and saw my juices dripping down her chin.

"Release me, please," I whispered desperately in between each pant of breath. "I wanna touch you, taste you. Let me go."

"No, bella," Anais tormented lovingly. "You're in trouble now." She flipped me over and began to eat my pussy in a way no one ever had, flitting my clitoris rapidly with her tongue while thrusting her middle finger into my pussy. I wriggled uncontrollably. All at once I wanted to pull away and push Anais further into my crotch. Anais tongued my clitoris and fingered me with increasing vigor until I squirted milky white cum. She licked it up and continued to enthusiastically stimulate my clit and g-spot while I shuddered wildly with orgasmic spasms. She made me cum another two times before finally relenting. She then ran her fingertips lightly over my torso and breasts while I, sweating and wheezing in excitement, caught my breath.

Anais pulled herself up towards my face. She loosened the rope while she kissed me intensely. I tried to mount her but she stopped me. "No, it's okay, bella. This wasn't about me. It was about you."

"But I want to please you," I pouted with disappointment.

"Oh you did. I came twice just watching you shake." She licked my lips. "You are exquisite, mami, and don't let anyone tell you otherwise."

We held one another, so caught up in the moment that neither noticed that Fabian had awoken and had been filming us.

6

I opened my eyes sleepily and squinted trying to force my eyes to adjust to the bright sunlight shining through the bay windows. I smiled, remembering the night, and extended my arm, expecting to feel Anais's soft skin. I groped the silk sheets but came up empty. I opened my eyes fully and looked around the room. Anais was nowhere to be found. Her clothes that had been lying on the red divan across the room were gone as well. I looked over at the chaise longue and saw that bare as well.

"Where is everyone?" I wondered.

I got up slowly and walked lazily to the bathroom. My pussy burned as I urinated; it felt like I had rug burn in my crotch.

"Ooooh," I winced loudly. "That bitch tore my pussy up," I

said laughing. "Put this ass to sleep."

I ran the shower and let the warm water cascade over my body. I touched my clit and shuddered, reminiscing about my encounter with Anais. Suddenly I felt a sharp pain in my side.

"Did you enjoy yourself, you fucking whore?!" asked Fabian furiously. He jabbed me in the ribs again and grabbed me by my hair. I struggled to break free. Before I could scream, Fabian punched me in the stomach and ribs, sending ripples of pain throughout my small frame and trapping my shriek in my throat. I collapsed into a heap. He pulled me to my knees by my hair and spat in my face. "What happened? I'm not good enough for you? I've never heard you scream like that when I fuck you? That bitch better than me? Huh? You fucking sucia!" He threw me down and spat at me again. He glowered at me pathetically as I balled myself into fetal position and sobbed quietly into my knees. "You fucking dyke!" he yelled as he threw a crumpled up sheet of paper at me. "Your lesbian lover left you a little note before she bounced. And she left you some money too, you fucking prostitute!" He threw the crumpled bills at me and stormed out.

I laid there rocking my bruised body. When I heard the front door slam, I leaned over and opened the wadded paper.

India,

You were amazing. I can't express how exquisitely you made me feel. I hope we can do this again. Next time, it must be just me and

WOMAN'S cry

you. Give me a call mi bella. 646-555-4608.

Besos,

Anais

*P.S. I'm leaving this money because it's <u>yours</u>. You gave it to me at the club but that money was given to you by your admirers. Buy yourself something nice and be sure to wear it for me on our next encounter. *wink wink**

I counted the money and was amazed to find almost six hundred dollars. I recalled giving Anais the money and the look of hesitation on her face. I giggled and was quickly brought back to my excruciating reality by the sharp pain in my abdomen. I sobbed quietly, cradling myself, wondering what the fuck it was going to take to break the fuck out of this abusive relationship.

**READ THE ENTIRE STORY IN THE NEW NOVEL,
WOMAN'S CRY BY VANESSA MARTIR.
IN STORES NOW...**

if it ain't one thing it's another

A NOVEL BY
SHARRON DOYLE

SNEAK PEEK

AUGUSTUS
PUBLISHING

chapter one

Share had just stepped out of the shower and was drying off when the phone rang. It was Petie. He was calling to let her know that he was on his way. Petie was a chocolate brotha with a six pack, a bunch of tattoos and a big dick. Yeah, he had a big gun. Share liked that.

She kept her feelings in check when it came to him or any other nigga. Niggas ain't shit but money and dick. Get on your knees and suck my clit. That was her motto, so catching feelings was a no-no.

Share remembered that she didn't douche. She had a variety of scents to choose from in her Summer's Eve selection: baby powder, vinegar and water, mountain rain and floral. She decided on mountain rain. She opened it up and swoosh-swoosh. She always felt good after a douche. Keep that booty hole fresh, girl, she said to herself.

Share went into the bedroom and smoothed White Diamonds lotion all over her body and then sprayed some between her legs. Fresh just for you, baby boy. She knew Petie would be there any minute, ready to beat it up. Just thinking about it made her body jump. She had a heartbeat down there and he hadn't even arrived yet. Damn, I'm open... slow down, breathe easy and remember he's only a play thing. She'd told herself that a number of times, but her body just wouldn't listen.

Petie called Share again to let her know that he had just parked the truck and to come downstairs and open the door for him. She'd thought about giving him keys, but she knew that would be the worst thing to do. That nigga would really think he was the boss if she did that. She let him be the boss in the bedroom; that was good enough.

Share didn't take orders or demands from anybody; she was the boss. But there was something about Petie that made her weak. And she was scared of her feelings when it came to him. He was only her back-breaker, she kept telling herself. That was it and that was all. But her emotions kept making her feel otherwise.

She knew he would be downstairs by now, so she threw on a spandex cat suit along with her favorite animal slippers and ran downstairs. Petie liked to see her in a cat suit, and he particularly liked the front, where it would cut between her pussy lips. Share had fat lips on her chocolate box, and right now she was ready for him to suck her sweets.

Petie waited patiently on the steps of Share's brownstone. She opened the door and stepped back into the foyer to let him in, and he gave her a pretty-ass smile that said, "You know I'm about to beat it." She loved that smile. And she knew all of his looks and what they meant too. She also knew she would have to dead it before he hurt her; Petie

was a heartbreaker who was not gonna leave his wife.

"What I told you about having me downstairs waiting like that? You know parole is looking for me," Petie said when they got upstairs.

"Baby, please, the warrant squad ain't out at night, so be easy," Share replied.

"Yeah, aiight." Petie took off his coat, threw it on a chair in the living room and made two drinks for them. She knew he liked to drink and argue before he got at her. He was on it like that. He would think of something to be angry about and then take it out on her in bed. She liked that rough shit, and she did all the things wifey didn't do. That's why his ass kept coming back.

The phone on her nightstand in the bedroom rang, and before Share could go and answer it, Petie rushed by her and snatched it up. "Speak. Who dis?" he barked. Petie waited impatiently for a few seconds to find out who was calling. Then he said, "Yeah, well, she's busy." And that was all Share heard before he pulled the phone's cord out of the wall. Here we go. Now he's got something to be angry about, she thought. "Come up out of that cat suit!" Petie called out before ordering her into the bedroom.

Petie placed his drink on the nightstand as Share entered the bedroom. The first thing she noticed was the phone on the floor. She stepped out of her cat suit and picked up the phone. Seeing the plug disconnected from the jack she said, "What the fuck you do to my phone?" Petie didn't answer. He had taken off his shirt and was coming out of his jeans now, giving her a 'You know what time it is' look. Damn, she loved that look. This nigga...ah, man, I'm feeling his gangsta, she thought.

Share never let Petie know how she truly felt about him, because then he would fuck everything up.

"Oh, you don't hear me now? I said, what the fuck you do to my phone?" "Nothing!" Petie pulled out the K-Y Jelly and began stroking himself. "Who the fuck is Will?" he finally said.

"A friend—and stop answering my phone. I don't answer your phone—do I?
All right then." She knew the more shit she popped the more intense their encounter would be, so she kept poppin' shit. And the more shit she popped the harder his dick got.

"You feeling brave tonight, huh...comin' out ya face. You gang-sta now, huh?" Petie said.

Share kept on and on. She got up in his grill, talking more shit. "Yeah, nigga, I'm feelin' gangsta—now what? Get it crunk!" she said, and he did. Before she could go on, Petie was biting her on the neck. He turned her around and started smacking his dick between her cheeks. He spit on her bumper and rubbed it on her hole. He called it his good-ness. "Ma, gimme my goodness," he'd say. But tonight he was taking it. It was all right, though. He could do that; it was his. Share never let anybody else hit her there. Petie rubbed his fingers around her entry, massaging the hole. Every now and then he would stick his tongue inside, just to get her more ready.

Petie was so smooth and despite his large sized penis, he nev-er ripped her. And he always talked her through it. "Share, put your thumb in your mouth," he said. "Yeah, like that. Now relax, ma, daddy got you. Don't run from me. Open up and let me in...yeah, that's what's

up. Gimme my goodness."

She felt him moving in deeper. "Ooh, God, Petie...please," she moaned. The head was the worst part, but once that got in it was a wrap. Share was on the floor on all fours with her back arched, her bumper at Petie's waist level. But the more he pushed, the lower she got. He continued stroking, and her butt began making juices, allowing him to easily slide in and out of her.

Share climbed onto the bed and Petie followed, hitting her like he was on a hang glider. He was giving her full pressure now, and it was his turn to pop shit. "So who the fuck is Will, huh?" stroking her deeper each time he asked.

"Aaah, Petie, please wait. Be nice," Share begged.

"Tell Will to lose your number, ya heard?" he said digging his gun deeper into her hole.

Oh, God, help me, Share thought. She couldn't take it anymore. It felt like he was making a new hole that wasn't supposed to be there. She fell flat on her stomach, hoping his gun would slip out—it didn't. Petie was long and strong and when she fell, he fell right with her; there was no escaping...in and out, in and out.

Share began to cry out. Petie loved that shit. The more she cried and moaned, the harder he stroked her. She just didn't know that all that crying made his dick even harder.

"Share, be quiet. Why are you making me punish you like this, huh? Answer me, ma." He was taunting her now. If she didn't answer right away he would go even deeper, and Share knew it.

"I don't know. I'm sorry," she whined. He stroked her long and easy now.

He spread her bumper cheeks so he could slide his whole self inside her. "Aaah, God, Petie...please, please."

"Please what, ma? Huh, please what? Answer me." Before Share could respond, she was coming all over the place. Her pussy cat was soaking wet; it was like a waterfall. God, this nigga is gonna make me crazy, she thought.

Petie's breathing quickened and he was stroking her long and hard again. He re-applied pressure, this time creating smacking noises each time he thrust himself inside of her. He pulled out and thrust himself back into her over and over again, until he finally fell on top of her, out of breath and kissing the back of her neck. "Whew! That's what's up, ma," he said. He rolled off of her, gave her a long kiss, wiped the sweat off her face and then kissed her nose. Share turned over onto her back, crossed her legs and looked over at Petie. After a few moments she got up, grabbed her hairbrush from off the dresser and swept her hair back; Petie had sweated out her doobie.

Share walked to the living room and took Petie's phone out of his coat pocket. She checked the missed calls to see if she recognized any of the numbers. Ha! Wifey had called only about three hundred times. She wished she knew his password so she could hear the messages. Don't worry; I'm sending him home now, bitch, she thought. She hated the idea of him leaving to go home to her. She wondered if he dug wifey out the same way he did her. The thought made her sick. She knew who his wife was, but his wife didn't know who she was. She put the phone back in his pocket after erasing all of the missed calls. He didn't need to know that she'd called so many times. Shit, he was going home to her.

Share fixed herself a drink and sat on the couch naked, waiting for Petie to come out of the bedroom. She thought that maybe they could swing another episode. Petie walked into the living room putting on his shirt. He looked at Share, wanting to get at her again, but there was no more time for that now; he knew wifey had probably blown his phone up. He bent down in front of Share, spread her legs and sucked on her sweets. She wrapped her legs around his neck, and he nibbled and licked on her clitoris until she was fully arched. He finally gave her one last suck before getting up and kissing her long and deep, their tongues entwined. "Next time, ma," Petie said kissing her nose. He reached for his coat and let himself out of the apartment. Share threw on a robe and ran downstairs to watch him walk to his truck. Yeah, next time, baby boy, she thought. Damn, I'm caught up with this nigga. Share's emotions were all over the place. It'll be all right...next time.

chapter TWO

Petie jumped in his truck and grabbed DMX's It's Dark and Hell Is Hot CD. He popped it into his CD player and pulled off, with How's It Goin' Down pumping out of his speakers. He always played that before and after seeing Share.

Petie knew Share was whipped. He put it on all the chicks like that. Nobody was special—not even wifey. He only stayed with her because of the kids. She was home base. Nobody could touch that, and he refused to let it go. She took care of his sons and cooked meals every night. Nah, he wasn't going anywhere. What wifey didn't know wouldn't hurt her. But if it wasn't for his sons he would've been bounced. She wasn't fun in the bedroom anymore. She was boring—unlike Share. Share was creative and always willing, and she took it in the bumper. Yeah, that's what he liked. Share was his, and if he ever found out somebody else was hitting that, he'd beat her down. However, there'd be

none of that; he knew she enjoyed that bedroom punishment. But if he ever caught her cheating, there'd be no enjoyment whatsoever—believe that.

Petie checked his phone and was surprised to see that wifey didn't call. That was strange. He pulled up to his building, shut the system off and hopped out of the truck. The regular cats were out front, waiting for the heads to come through. That's how it was in the hood—always on the paper chase. Family gotta eat, bills gotta be paid and muthafuckas don't want to hire convicted felons.... Get that money; it's yours for the taking.

Petie put the key in the door, hoping that wifey would be asleep. But something told him she'd be up waiting for him with a million questions. He walked into his sons' bedroom and looked in on them. They were fast asleep...his little men. He loved them to death. That's what kept him coming home every night.

Petie took off his coat and went to the bedroom to see if his wife, Renee, was awake. She was. She gave him a 'Where you been?' look. He pulled off his G-Units and lined them up with the other twenty-six pairs of kicks he had. Petie had different footwear for every day of the month. You name it, he had it, and he made sure his little men had it too.

Petie kissed Renee on the cheek, and she began with the million questions. "Where you been? Why didn't you call? Why you look like that? Why you always gotta go out at night? What took you so long? Who was you with? Was you with a bitch? Why you lyin'?" Damn, she's nosy. He wanted to be rid of her ass, but he wouldn't do that to his sons.

Renee was a good mother. He couldn't take that away from her. She had homemaker skills. She took care of the house and devoted all of her time to their sons. He couldn't break up his happy home.

Petie remembered growing up and watching his mother struggle and work two jobs to make ends meet. She had a hard life, and he always wondered as a boy why his father just upped and left the way he did. He thought his pops didn't love him. Petie remembered how unwanted and neglected he felt as a child without his father...all the other kids doing things with their dads and his was nowhere around. He had abandoned him and left him to grow up without him. He hated him for that, and he vowed that he would never cause his little men that kind of pain—never; so if it meant that he was stuck with Renee for life, then so be it. He was determined to have his sons grow up with both of their parents. He lived for them since they were born. They were all that mattered...his little men. But here he was being interrogated again, as usual. It was a no-win situation.

Petie snatched off his clothes down to his boxers and got in the bed. He took the remote control and turned on some porno. He had to watch the porno channel just to get in the mood to be with Renee. It just wasn't the same anymore; she no longer excited him, so he would watch the chicks on the screen and imagine that he was hitting them instead.... Damn, one chick looked like Desiree...yeah, Des. Petie was thinking about going to check her tomorrow. She was a head nurse fa sho. After taking the boys to school, he'd spin past her crib so she could polish his gun. But in the meantime, he was in bed with wifey who didn't even make him brick anymore.... She wouldn't

even wear thongs; she wore briefs. He couldn't understand why she had become so boring. There was no chemistry between them anymore. Petie reached over and put his hand on her thigh. "Petie, I'm not in the mood," she said. She kissed him on the cheek and rolled over.

"Goodnight," she added.

"Goodnight, ma. I love you," Petie replied.

"Yeah, I love you, too."

Petie lay there for a few moments and cut off the TV. No problem; he could go to bed brick tonight. He wasn't in the mood for her anyway. No sweat off his back. He would go see Des in the morning and then go and check Alexis. He had it all planned. Yeah, I need my sleep anyway, he thought looking over at Renee.

**READ THE ENTIRE STORY IN THE NEW NOVEL,
IF IT AIN'T ONE THING IT'S ANOTHER BY SHARRON DOYLE.
IN STORES NOW...**

Hard White: On the street of New York only on color matters
Novel By Anthony Whyte Based on the screenplay by Shannon Holmes

The streets are pitch black...A different shade of darkness has drifted to the North Bronx neighborhood known as Edenwald. Sleepless nights, there is no escaping dishonesty, disrespect, suspicion, ignorance, hostility, treachery, violence, karma... Hard White metered out to the residents. Two, Melquan and Precious have big dreams but must overcome much in order to manifest theirs. Hard White the novel is a story of triumph and tribulations of two people's journey to make it despite the odds. Nail biting drama you won't ever forget...Once you pick it up you can't put it down. Deftly written by Anthony Whyte based on the screenplay by Shannon Holmes, the story comes at you fast, furiously offering an insight to what it takes to get off the streets. It shows a woman's unWlimited love for her man. Precious is a rider and will do it all again for her man, Melquan... His love for the street must be bloodily severed. Her love for him will melt the coldest heart...Together their lives hang precariously over the crucible of Hard White. Read the novel and see why they make the perfect couple.

$14.95 // 9780982541531

When Love Turns To Hate
By Sharron Doylee

Petie is back regulating from down south. He rides with a new ruthless partner, and they're all about making fast money. The partners mercilessly go after a shady associate who is caught in an FBI sting and threatens their road to riches. Petie and his two sons have grown apart. Renee, their mother, has to make a big decision when one of her sons wild-out. Desperately, she tries to keep her world from crumbling while holding onto what's left of her family. Venus fights for life after suffering a brutal physical attack. Share goes to great lengths to make sure her best friend's attacker stays ruined forever. Crazy entertaining and teeming with betrayal, corruption, and murder, When Love Turns To Hate is mixed with romance gone awry. The drama will leave you panting for more....

$14.95 // 9780982541517

Street Chic
By Anthony Whyte

A new case comes across the desk of detective Sheryl Street, from the Dade county larceny squad in Miami. Pursuing the investigation she discovers that it threatens to unfold some details of her life she thought was left buried in the Washington Heights area of New York City. Her duties as detective pits her against a family that had emotionally destabilized her. Street ran away from a world she wanted nothing to do with. The murder of a friend brings her back as law and order. Surely as night time follows daylight, Street's forced into a resolve she cannot walk away from. Loyalty is tested when a deadly choice has to be made. When you read this dark and twisted novel you'll find out if allegiance to her family wins Street over. A most interesting moral conundrum exists in the dramatic tension that is Street Chic.

$14.95 // 9780932541500

SMUT central
By Brandon McCalla

Markus Johnson, so mysterious he barely knows who he is. An infant left at the doorstep of an orphanage. After fleeing his refuge, he was taken in by a couple with a perverse appetite for sexual indiscretions, only to become a star in the porn industry... Dr. Nancy Adler, a shrink who gained a peculiar patient, unlike any she has ever encountered. A young African American man who faints upon sight of a woman he has never met, having flashbacks of a past he never knew existed. A past that contradicts the few things he knows about himself... Sex and lust tangled in a web so disgustingly tantalizing and demented. Something evil, something demonic... Something beyond the far reaches of a porn stars mind, peculiar to a well established shrink, leaving an old NYPD detective on the verge of solving a case that has been a dead end for years... all triggered by desires for a mysterious woman...

$14.95 // 9780982541586

Dead And Stinkin'
By Stephen Hewett

A collection of three deadly novellas, Dead and Stinkin' invokes the themes of Jamaican folklore and traditions West Indian storytelling in a modern setting.

$14.95 // 9780982541555

Power of the P
By James Hendricks

Erotica at its gritty best, Power of the P is the seductive story of an entrepreneur who wields his powerful status in unimaginable — and sometimes unethical — ways. This exotic ride through the underworld of sex and prostitution in the hood explores how sex is leveraged to gain advantage over friends and rivals alike, and how sometimes the white collar world and the streets aren't as different as we thought they were.

$14.95 / / 9780982541579

America's Soul
By Erick S Gray

Soul has just finished his 18-month sentence for a parole violation. Still in love with his son's mother, America, he wants nothing more than for them to become a family and move on from his past. But while Soul was in prison, America's music career started blowing up and she became entangled in a rocky relationship with a new man, Kendall. Kendall is determined to keep his woman by his side, and America finds herself caught in a tug of war between the two men. Soul turns his attention to battling the street life that landed him in jail — setting up a drug program to rid the community of its tortuous meth problem — but will Soul's efforts cross his former best friend, the murderous drug kingpin Omega?

$14.95 / / 9780982541548

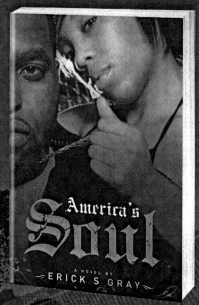

GHETTO GIRLS IV

Young Luv

Ghetto Girls IV Young Luv
$14.95 // 9780979281662

Ghetto Girls
$14.95 // 0975945319

Ghetto Girls Too
$14.95 // 0975945300

Ghetto Girls 3 Soo Ho
$14.95 // 0975945351

THE BEST OF THE STREET CHRONICLES TODAY, THE **GHETTO GIRLS SERIES** IS A WONDERFULLY HYPNOTIC ADVENTURE THAT DELVES INTO THE CONVOLUTED MINDS OF CRIMINALS AND THE DARK WORLD OF POLICE CORRUPTION. YET, THERE IS SOMETHING THRILLING AND SURPRISINGLY TENDER ABOUT THIS ONGOING YOUNG-ADULT SAGA FILLED WITH MAD FLAVA.

Love and a Gangsta
author // **ERICK S GRAY**

This explosive sequel to **Crave All Lose All**. Soul and America were together ten years 'til Soul's incarceration for drugs. Faithfully, she waited four years for his return. Once home they find life ain't so easy anymore. America believes in holding her man down and expects Soul to be as committed. His lust for fast money rears its ugly head at the same time America's music career takes off. From shootouts, to hustling and thugging life, Soul and his man, Omega, have done it. Omega is on the come-up in the drug-game of South Jamaica, Queens. Using ties to a Mexican drug cartel, Omega has Queens in his grip. His older brother, Rahmel, was Soul's cellmate in an upstate prison. Rahmel, a man of God, tries to counsel Soul. Omega introduces New York to crystal meth. Misery loves company and on the road to the riches and spoils of the game, Omega wants the only man he can trust, Soul, with him. Love between Soul and America is tested by an unforgivable greed that leads quickly to deception and murder.

$14.95 // 9780979281648

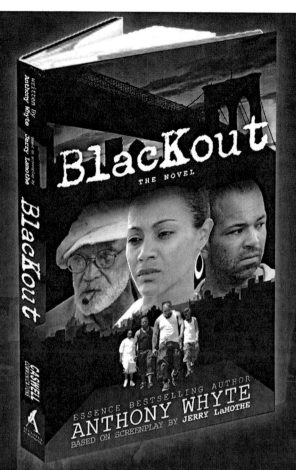

The lights went out
and the
mayhem began.

It's gritty in the city but hotter in Brooklyn where a small community in east Flatbush must come to grips with its greatest threat, self-destruction. August 14 and 15, 2003, the eastern section of the United States is crippled by a major shortage of electrical power, the worst in US history. Blackout, the spellbinding novel is based on the epic motion picture, directed by Jerry Lamothe. A thoroughly riveting story with delectable details of families caught in a harsh 48 hours of random violent acts, exploding in deadly conflict. There's a message in everything... even the bullet. The author vividly places characters on the stage of life and like pieces on a chess-board, expertly moves them to a tumultuous end. Voila! Checkmate, a literary triumph. Blackout is a masterpiece. This heart-stopping, page-turning drama is moving fast. Blackout is destined to become an American classic.

BASED ON SCREENPLAY BY **JERRY LaMOTHE**

Inspired by true events

US $14.95 CAN $20.95
ISBN 978-0-9820653-0-3

CASWELL
COMMUNICATIONS

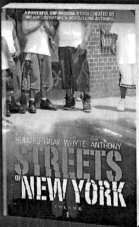 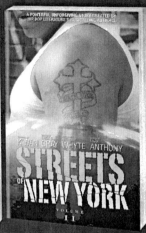 

CPSIA information can be obtained at www.ICGtesting.com
Printed in the USA
LVOW10s1436141015

458227LV00001B/1/P